SUGARHOUSE PETE

An American Family Story

Steven M. Berezney

SUGARHOUSE PETE
AN AMERICAN FAMILY STORY

iUniverse books may be ordered through booksellers or by contacting:

iUniverse
1663 Liberty Drive
Bloomington, IN 47403
www.iuniverse.com
844-349-9409

ISBN: 978-0-5953-9519-4 (sc)
ISBN: 978-0-5958-3918-6 (e)

Print information available on the last page.

iUniverse rev. date: 08/03/2020

This book is dedicated to my grandchildren
Julia, Jack, Leslie, Nicholas, Annika,
Steven, Elena and Anders.

Acknowledgements

Jack Fleming, a top sports announcer of football and basketball for West Virginia University, the Pittsburgh Steelers and Chicago Bulls. He was the first to encourage me to write a book about my father and family. Jack has passed away and I miss him. He was a special friend that I wish was here.

Many other friends read a draft and they were exuberant supporters. Lee and Lorraine Bracy were an immense help, as were Dr. Demie Mainieri and his wife Rosetta. My close friend Art MacLeod and I spent hours going over many chapters.

I want to tip my cap to Harvey Zucker, Managing Editor of the Jersey Journal, who made important suggestions. Reference librarians also rate recognition, especially Cynthia Harris of the New Jersey Room at the Jersey City Main Public Library. I also received help from Tim Mendoza of Authors Solutions and Leo Collins of iUniverse Publishing.

I owe a special thanks to my wife, Germaine, who reviewed each page with warm approval. I often called my son in law Janos Angeli to resolve a problem. I appreciate the support of my son Peter and my daughters Perianne and Stefanie. It was wonderful for them to be so willing to help.

Sugarhouse Pete

Table of Contents

"Sugarhouse Pete," my father and I in the 1960's.

1

Bright Street

I grew up on Bright Street in Jersey City during the Great Depression. It was not like Main Street, where the America dream was realized, far from it.

The name suggested something better, but only the word survival described the decade. The nation was in the midst of a severe economic collapse as disruptive to the fears of everyday living on the poor as it was for the wealthy.

Most of the families where I lived were low income earners trying to survive the depression. Despite being poor they were friendly, but hid the problems of the harshness on a day to day living.

It was a time for worrying in America.

An interesting footnote is that Bright Street was near Paulus Hook, Jersey City's first settlement. George Washington ordered an attack to capture a British Fort in the community, who ruled the area during the Revolutionary War. The skirmish was repelled in a bitter setback, except historians said it boosted American morale.

The only evidence that remains of Paulus Hook is a plaque on a waterfront office building, except no one cared about colonial events of the 1930's that had no bearing on their lives.

My parents were average occupants of Bright Street. My father had a job, but barely made enough money to pay for the rent and food we needed. My mother was a typical housewife tending to my father, five sons and our rooms in that order. My father worried about what would happen to his family, if he lost his job. My mother had a more positive attitude and worried about nothing except my father.

Their lives together began in America following separate journeys from Eastern Europe. They met and married in Jersey City where they put down roots. They liked all the city could offer, but it was different to get use to from the rural, mountain environment they knew.

My mother was content until the country fell into a severe economic decline. After the Stock Market crashed, many businesses failed that caused the loss of an enormous number of jobs. The events led her to be as concerned as my father, but now she understood why he worried about the possibility of losing his job.

The Depression was a ruinous tyrant.

When the Depression got worse and workers had their pay cut, sometimes by half their earnings, poverty set in on Bright Street, across Jersey City and all of New Jersey, New York and the nation.

Laid off workers were left destitute without any income that resulted in their evictions. Soon farmers were without funds to pay their mortgages, adding to the Depression. My brothers John and Mike were anxious to help the family, but there were few jobs for young bucks. Paul was eager to join in the task but he was in high school. Pete got a summer job driving a truck with items of steel for various projects. My first job was at the American Can Company. It was noisy and my small earnings didn't add much to help our family, but the gesture was real.

My father had his own escape mechanism. It was similar to a secret he had of his bed in Europe. He didn't earn enough money with or without it, but it eased his doubts. If he lost his job, he would forget the bed and become a farmer. He would boast about his experience tending a vegetable garden that led him to believe he could grow the food we needed, as he did in the "old country." The prospect of becoming a farmer was only wishful thinking to soothe away any worry, especially for my mother.

The scariest time was when unemployment reached twenty five percent. It was a frightening figure that threatened the country beyond what the statistics indicated that left the nation in despair. So many were out of work for so long there seemed to be no way to cope with their struggles, but the worse situation was some of the jobless were forced to live in tin shacks on a kind of no man's land outside city limits called "Hoovervilles." The shacks were a troubling sight that produced the most apt phrase to describe the decade.

It was hard times.

An encouraging announcement was to go West. President Roosevelt indicted the massive fear the dire economy created and his programs rallied the country. In many ways he succeeded, but it took the build up to World War II and our entry into the war. The growth in jobs the country needed completed the recovery.

Seeing the tin shacks made me grateful we lived on Bright Street, but people said if you drove down the street slowly, you would not miss a thing. The residents had more serious problems to concern them and ignored idle opinions.

An elementary school was in the middle of the block showing its wear, as were several two family wood houses between tenements across the street from the school in need of repair. I was born on the second floor of one of the houses and have been on the run ever since, trying to catch up with what everyone called a rushed birth.

With two churches, a school, a grocery, a candy store, two movie theatres, a large library and a small park were all within walking distance of Bright Street. It was a prime example of what people today call a "village." Women would congregate at the grocery ready with a wide range of information, including where to find bargain clothes, especially for children and a men's jacket.

The gatherings were before the term "village" was used to describe the unity that existed in small rural towns, but areas like Bright Street would fit the description. To add to the unusual makeup of Bright Street, there was a horse stable at the far corner of the Street.

The stable provided an important service for peddlers, who sold their useful wares from horse drawn wagons. It was a shelter for the horses to rest and feed them. An odor was emitted from the stable that was far from a common experience in the city. You can guess how some residents felt about it. I often played in the stable's loft, as well as in the horse stalls, where remnants of manure ended up on my clothing.

The stable was different from my normal playtime venue of empty lots, but my mother knew where I had been as soon as I came home. She quickly separated me from my clothing to scrub wash them. It was a strenuous chore, but a vital one, except I ignored her warnings not to go into the horse stalls.

I loved the neighborhood, but what energized me was the time I spent with four older brothers. They created a special optimism where something was always happening, both good and bad. They were involved with women, jobs, school, cars and sports that made my growing up a happy experience, especially my time with my brother John.

He was my oldest brother followed by Mike, Paul and Pete. There were five years between Pete and I, but seventeen years separated me from John, sixteen years from Mike and eleven years from Paul. In many ways, John was like a father figure, but the age difference between us was too great for me to cross over into his world. I longed for the time when we could do adult things together.

John had an "all for the family" comitment that seemed to help us out of financial problems when we needed it the most. I often heard my parents talk about their struggles to pay bills. It was a constant discourse between them during the Depression.

At a critical time, John got a job at a shipyard in Kearny for $8 dollars a week, just before my father's pay was cut. John gave most of it to my mother to help pay bills. It was a small amount of money by today's standards, but she said it "saved our family."

There were occasional reports of someone who was able to climb above economic problems through luck or grit, but mostly the only move anyone on Bright Street made was to go "on relief." It was program to provide a small amount of financial aid, but many considered it a last resort they tried to avoid.

The contradiction is hard to accept, but there were some people who did not want to admit to being so desperate. As foolish as it may seem, a person's pride remained the last line of defence against economic problems, especially during the early years of the Depression.

Fortunately, we never went on relief.

Another phrase we often heard was to "hang in there." It was a firm verbal encouragement to remain steadfast against economic pressures. The term seemed to sum up the era, as much as it did "hard times." It was a sincere attempt to help someone overcome concerns of unemployment or debt, often both. Everyone was grateful for the support and it became a common expression, even over trivial matters. One thing, the economy was not the worse difficulty my family had to face.

A more heartless problem entered our lives when my mother lapsed into mental depression. It became an overwhelming hardship that dwarfed the impact of our financial needs. Finding the right words to describe her illness was difficult, especially over something so personal and inadequate of details. She was never incoherent, only withdrawn and despondent with a concern that was beyond what we ever imagined.

It seemed we were about to lose our optimism, as if some force was trying to pull it away from us when we needed it the most. With her near constant silence, it was difficult to help her. The problem was we didn't know what to do, but challenged why she had lost her strength. Some people say a price must be paid for happiness with tragedy. Well, we got more than what we felt was our share of misfortune. Pills didn't work, but she liked it when my father and brothers were with her. For us to try to be normal was never easy. John's advice was just to be pleasant. She also liked it when neighbors came to visit her.

A medical review was diagnosed as a "change of life," a critical impact on the inner self. My mother's illness left my father with his own despair. The medical help proscribed seemed to be the same as another doctor to be patient, except it was a slow, intermittent process. Ultimately, her problem left as quiet as when it arrived. One day, she laughed over someone's passing comment and we laughed with her.

We took it as a good sign.

She never wanted to talk about her illness, and we never asked her about it, except for the movies. She loved Cowboy Westerns. My father didn't, but he helped and took her to see them. As she grew stronger, we took her for quiet walks that seemed to gradually help her improve.

The episode took a path to recovery from the movies and when my father asked my mother to dance to a slow Polka, my mother smiled and danced, but they sat down after a few twirling moves. Thew would talk to each other quietly like husband and wife.

2
The Decision

It was early 1905 in a remote mountain area of Eastern Europe when the decision was made for my father to leave home and go to America.

His home was in a small village called Terschana on the north side of the Carpathian Mountains as a part of the Austro-Hungarian Empire. The village was similar to hundreds of others like it, except my father was not Austrian, Hungarian or Polish.

He was a Rusyn, an obscure people to most Americans, but with a history that can be traced back over a thousand to three thousand years. They were peasants without a country living on both sides of the Carpathian Mountains, a renowned range to Rusyns and Eastern Europeans. They were an energetic people destined to a life of poverty, who worked on small plots of land for crops to sustain them, but also to sell them.

It was a misty day when the plan that would change his life was decided, but he did not know his going to America had been approved by his parents, his sister and priest to support the journey. He was out early to do his chores, but the rain created a chill that made him think of his warm bed and not a journey across an ocean. A passing neighbor interrupted my father's thoughts that made it a day he would remember forever.

"You go to America. Good. It's good you go."

The simple words were said without emotion in the syntax of their language, but the impact of the meaning shook him from his reverie. His departure had been discussed for several months, but he was opposed to the plan to sail across an ocean.

He shivered from the cold mist, but also from the thought of a long sea voyage. Despite the opportunities everyone said America offered, he did not want to leave his parents or his home. He could not speak of it. Speaking English troubled him, but crossing an ocean was a close second. He did not know which was worse, but felt both were worrisome prospects he had to resolve.

There was also the question of his age.

He was fifteen years old when his father said he had to go to America without him and his mother. He had many negative reactions to leaving home, but mostly he felt he was being rushed to manhood faster than he wanted to get there. An older brother and sister were in America and felt sure they would help him. He thought if they could make the journey, he could too, but a nagging issue troubled him.

It was a simple attempt he contrived with his bed to oppose an edict for him to leave home. His bed became a mental crutch that represented the security of his home. At his age, he needed something to overcome his doubts, and nothing had more meaning to him than his parents, his home and his bed.

The bed was a unique sought after place to sleep in poor, rural homes' It was in the kitchen on a sturdy shelf above the oven. It is hard to imagine, but the berth made it the warmest place to sleep on cold nights. His feeling about it was easy to understand. It was referred to as a comfortable niche, but his father was not about to let anything interfere with the prospect of his youngest son going to America, least of all a bed.

The trek would not be across a nearby border, but to a faraway land. It started with a journey through Poland to Germany, where he would board a ship to cross the Atlantic Ocean in steerage class that offered no amenities. It was a crowded and unpleasant experience, especially after the ship encountered a storm that extended the voyage to nearly ten days, twice the usual time to cross the Atlantic.

The passengers in steerage suffered the most, but if my father had known the possibility of a storm, he would never have left his home and the world he knew. He thought a storm at sea would have been all he needed to convince his father not to send him on a journey to America.

Several problems were created. The first was the smell of urine from children peeing in their beds, plus a foul odor from badly maintained toilets. A more threatening reaction was when the storm hit the ship. The air vents in steerage were shut, and the passengers were prevented from going on deck. The only indignity they did not suffer was to be chained to their beds, but it did not matter they were imprisoned by their fears.

After being shut up an entire day, my father could not tolerate the confinement any longer. Despite warnings of the danger he went to go on deck. A ship's officer confronted him on a stairway. He ordered him back, but a crowd had gathered shouting "give us air" in several languages, adding to the tension. My father's attempt to escape the discomfort was unnecessary.

A ship officer pointed to several overhead vents he intended to have opened, as soon as the seamen arrived. When fresh air came gushing into steerage, the ship's passengers cheered their relief, ignoring the water that splashed down on them.

One question remained. Why weren't the vents opened to let fresh air into steerage? The problem should have been attended to sooner, but immigrant passengers had little authority to eliminate a problem. After the vents were opened, the passengers credited my father for their relief. Several immigrants called him a hero, but he could not understand the remark.

He said he only wanted to get fresh air.

I have smiled every time I heard the story about his confrontation with a ship's officer. It was not what you would expect from a youthful teenager, who was not the saviour type, but he could not have done otherwise at any age, whether he was fifteen or fifty. It was an early example of his trying to correct a simple wrong.

My brother John often told me my father was always proud to describe his history as a Carpatho-Rusyn, but it disturbed him to talk about being a disadvantaged and oppressed people, who never established a country of their own.

Overrun in their history by Tartars, Poles, Hungarians and Austrians, Rusyns challenged each invasion. Despite valiant efforts, they were unable to repel their harsh intruders, but the people endured. Rusyns still live in the area of the Carpathian Mountains, mostly in Poland, Slovakia, Romania, Serbia, Hungary and the United States.. It is hard to establish the total number of Rusyns in America, but estimates indicate it at 700,000.

As a tribute to their heritage and to define their ancestors, a dedicated group of Rusyns created a new national organization called the Carptho-Rusyn Society. It was formed in Pittsburgh, Pa. in 1994 to expand the knowledge of Rusyns as a unique people over looked in America and Eastern Europe. New memberships have been promoted throughout both areas.

Carpathian Rusyn Map, 2004

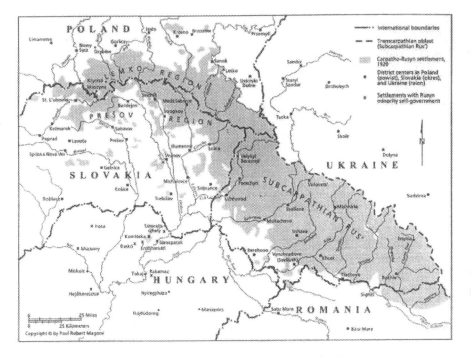

The shaded portion on the map represents the Carpatian—
Rusyn areas in Eastern Europe. My parents are from the
Lemko Region in southern Poland, north of the mountains.
The map is from the book, "Our People Carpatho-
Rusyns" by Dr. Paul Robert Magocsi and displayed with
the permission of the Carpatho-Rusyn Research Center.

An important historical development occurred with the acquisition and control of most of Eastern Europe by the Austro-Hungarian Empire. It stabilized the region, but the new rulers were tough minded despots. Their oppression continued until Franz Joseph became the Emperor and instituted positive changes to help the people. His acts endeared him to all Ruyns and they responded by calling him: "The Savior."

World War I brought new hardships when Rusyns were drafted into the Austrian army, but suffered their harshest fate following World War II. Polish officials charged Rusyns from the Lemko Region with aiding Ukraine in an attempt to gain independence from the Soviet Union. Many families were forced to abandon their homes to work on farms in Ukraine. The move was promoted as a voluntary act by Polish and Russian officials, but that position has been strongly contested.

Poland was under strict control of the USSR and Rusyns feel the episode was Communist managed. The facts are clear and the move has been condemned as indefensible on humanitarian and moral grounds. It is referred to as the Vistula Operation, after the river in the area of the event. Rusyns believe it was an unlawful action that remains unresolved.

Spread across many borders by a mountain range, Rusyns have maintained a unified spirit, but they were never able to do more than eke out a paltry existence against the forces of nature and circumstance to survive on small plots of land. They persevered, growing simple crops, such as potatoes, beets and red cabbage. To have a cow or a horse was a luxury, and few owned either one. Some tended sheep, but whatever they did, it was hard to sustain a family.

Early records are sketchy, but Rusyns would have been listed far below the recorded economic averages of most Europeans. They faced a harsh reality with little hope for a better future. Without any governmental authority, they relied on their Orthodox Christian faith and their priests to guide them. To demonstrate their commitment, they built large wood churches to testify to their devotion, many on hilltops.

Their priests helped secure loans for immigrant sons and daughters to go to America, but over time, the clergy became a part of the upper class and few changes were instituted to bring about the economic improvements the people needed to ease their poverty. They realized they could only count on their labor to sustain them, but many doubted it.

Too often, it was not enough.

Rusyns did not have to be reminded of how poor they were, but an encouraging opportunity would change their lives as it did for many others throughout Europe. With the advance of industry a great number of workers were needed in America from European immigrants. They were aided to make the journey and work in a new Country in steel mills and coal mines.

Many Eastern Europeans who migrated to America were penniless, but helped by relatives who arrived before them. They needed a ticket even for steerage class. The migration continued into 1924. In some cases, it was extended to 1930, when the open door policy to America ended.

My father fit the example of most immigrants who made the journey early in the 1900's. He was poor from a needy family, but despite his age his father said it was time for his youngest son to take advantage of what America offered. A plan was set up for him to work in a coal mine in Pennsylvania with a man from his village, who migrated a decade earlier. My father knew nothing about coal mining, except it would be different from a vegetable garden.

Immigrants on his ship could not believe he had a job, despite it being in a coal mine. Physically mature with strong arms, he had a will from his father and was ready for any kind of labor. Mostly he was happy he would be working in America with a fellow Rusyn from his village.

The days before he had to leave were difficult. One morning, he arose early from his bed, but hesitated to eat breakfast. His mother quickly settled his indecision and told him to do his chores. There was a misty rain falling, but he saw his father and hurried to him. He wanted to make a final attempt to convince him not to leave home.

The outdoor meeting was an unusual setting for a serious discussion, but it did not make it less important. His father complained about the cold. The weather was not what he wanted to discuss and argued with his father. It prompted him to mention his bed, but his father dismissed that subject. It left him indecisive, without knowing what to say. His father reminded him the decision for him to go to America was settled. He could only repeat that he wanted to stay home.

"To do what," his father asked?

It was a challenging question he could not answer, but knew he had to accept the decision to go to America. Actually, his father understood his son's concern, but told him many young men from their village had left to go to America and more was sure to follow, including whole families. It was what my father wanted to hear and it encouraged him to suggest that his parents should go to America with him.

"Come with me, Poppa," he urged.

"No, I'm too old, and your mother would never leave, so no more talk about it," he replied.

His father was always direct in what he wanted done and this meeting was no exception. His words were brisk in tone and manner that left no room for argument. My father's problem was a simple one. He loved his parents and his home and did not want to live another kind of life without them.

He thought his father would need him, but he felt a pang of loneliness if had to leave. He knew he had no choice than to obey his father's wishes. He would be going on one of life's long journeys, one he would have to make alone and not just to America.

My father's feeling about the promises of America was obvious, but he was too young to grasp its benefits. He worried over what would happen to him, but never mentioned it. After meeting with his father, he developed another plan. When he earned enough money, he would bring his mother to America. He was sure his father would follow them, but that idea was never a possibility.

He went to finish his chores, but could not quell his anxiety. He only wished his father had been more understanding, as he tended his family's small garden, thinking about the thought of crossing an ocean. The vegetable garden was easy to maintain. He described it as only needing a little amount of attention, but it was important. He wondered who would care for it when he was gone'

When he went back to his house, he thought about the time he had before he would have to leave. It was not long. His mother knew to the minute, but never spoke of it. She did not discuss family matters openly, but he did not know she worried about his leaving home, except he lacked her stoicism. If he had known her feelings, he might have opposed his father in a more deliberate way.

Knowing the time for him to leave was near, he wanted to be with his mother as much as possible. He was not hungry for the breakfast she gave him It was dark hard bread with hot tea that burned when he drank it. He liked it that way, but ate more bread to ease the hot tea. He loved the bread, but not in the same way he loved his mother.

She was the bread of his life.

Thoughts of his mother's tea and bread stayed with him as simple reminders of his love for his parents and his home. Lasting memories are often created out of such moments. Somehow, they sum up life's loving experiences, regardless of how trivial they are in our lives. They are simple occurrences of love a family can share and often do.

In time, he realized his father's effort to send him to America was the right decision. He would say he was a practical man. Later, when he learned of their passing, first his father and later his mother, he was sad and thought of the day he left home. They lived a long life, but he never saw them again.

3

The Journey

The wagon came early in the morning.

It was an open cart with a driver in front and seats in back. There were four males making the journey, including my father and a cousin he never met before. He was thirty years old, but hardly mentioned in family discussions. An adult relative was required for anyone making the voyage to America, who was not seventeen years of age. His cousin would be his guardian, but he had a bragging attitude my father did not like.

As it turned out he was feeble support.

My father was the last one picked up, but a youth from a nearby village was also making the journey with his uncle, a quiet man who spoke little. He was the opposite of the young man's exuberant personality, who greeted my father warmly. The wagon would take them through Poland for a train connection to the German border.

It was moren enough time to become friends.

With his mother's help, my father packed a small bag with the usual necessities. They included ankle high shoes his father gave him, as well as his favorite jacket, plus a heavy sweater and a pair of trousers. The shoes were too good to wear on the ship that he put in the bag, but he wore his best cap.

He included several pairs of socks, two shirts, and an extra pair of "long johns" in anticipation of it being cold at sea. It may have been his most practical item on the voyage. He had not started shaving, so he did not pack a razor.

Some of his mother's food was added for the journey, including two loaves of bread, a bag of dark tea, some kielbasa and a small bottle of liquor that was a parting gesture from his father. The food would prove to be essential, as well as the liquor.

He was glad his father included it.

Lastly, his mother gave him several bars of the soap she felt he would need. She was a stickler for cleanliness and told him to bathe every day, eat her bread and drink the tea.

They were her parting words.

As the wagon prepared to leave, he embraced his mother, but he could not hold back his tears. He wiped them away then hugged his father. He felt like a boy trying to act like a man.

It was not an easy time.

The wagon made its way down the road, as he looked back to see his parents standing in a stoic pose of resignation with their arms raised in a parting gesture. He waved goodbye before they were gone from view, adding to his depressed feeling of leaving home. If going to America was a positive a adventure, he did not like it.

First, the route was a common on he would have to endure through Poland. It stopped at villages for two nights to allow him to sleep on his way to Germany. He was awake most of both nights trying to sleep on an uncomfortable cot that kept him awake. The second night was the same on a cot.

He was up early each day, but tired on the train to the German border. He wished he could have slept longer, except he was glad to be rid of the cots. His documents were approved and he hoped his seat would be comfortable to get some sleep.

At the border, he was content to remain quiet as his cousin was eager to answer questions for the immigration officials, but glad when the session was over. Several documents were issued that he would need on the journey, but he had an indifferent attitude toward them. He boarded the train for the port city of Hamburg on the Elbe River and his ship to America.

He took a seat next to the window, which he felt would be restful. His guardian, who he did not like, sat several rows from him drinking liquor. The rocking of the train made him weary and he slept most of the way. It was dawn when he awoke to see everyone staring out a window at the city of Hamburg. His reaction was it was a large city.

A short time later, he was interviewed again by several immigration officials, including his cousin. It was a formal session with many questions compared to the border, except there was a problem. His cousin was half drunk and making no sense. My father was sure they would not be approved to make the voyage, and he would have to return home to explain what happened. He didn't want to do that. Not now, not after he had overcome a great deal of emotional distress. He felt his father would send him on another ship to America, a prospect he did not want to do. again

Once was enough for him.

There was only one option left and he took it. He was not a speech maker, but he knew he had to defend himself. He found his voice and told the officials he was a strong worker, who would be good for America. He offered a similar report for his cousin, blaming his drinking on the rigors of the long journey.

His response proved to be significant.

The translator related his plea to other officials and papers were stamped he was sure were his rejection, but were his approval to sail to America, including his cousin. He felt a wave of confidence and laughed and cried at the same time, as he did when he was overjoyed. Several days before, he was unhappy over leaving home, but his presentation enabled him to make the voyage, despite his doubts to cross an ocean.

Following the interview, his guide led the group to an old hotel near the waterfront. It had seen many travellers that left it worn out, but typical of the Germans it was neat and clean. He shared a room, but it had a comfortable bed that pleased him. That night he went out to a local bar with other passengers, including several Rusyns who were anxious to celebrate their good fortune.

He had never been in a bar before and loved the environment. His description of it was unrestrained. He said he appreciated the bar, but liked German beer more. Feeling exuberant, he picked up a pitcher to drink from instead of a mug, as an example of his new confidence. Everyone cheered, but it disturbed the bartender, who rushed to stop his drinking from the pitcher and challenged his age. His friends lied and assured him he was old enough, but he had to use the mug to drink beer and not the pitcher.

Everyone laughed, including my father.

Some German patrons joined the festivities. They understood the reach of the Austro-Hungarian Empire and knew it included the areas on both sides of the Carpathian Mountain, as far to the East as Ukraine and Romania. At times, he had been referred to as Austrian and only nod, but he was anxious to explain his Rusyn heritage.

The Germans understood his history, except they insisted Rusyns were Austrians and their cousins. The comingling created a friendly environment, but they had to limit their communication to simple words and hand signs. They laughed at the feeble efforts to converse in different languages, as if it was a game of charades.

In less than a decade, they would be involved in another contest that would not be a word game, but a disastrous war. Fortunately, my mother and father were in America during World War I supporting the Allies. They had two children with my mother expecting a third. When the war was over, America had earned the recognition as a major world power.

Rusyns would never refer to themselves as Austrians again, except in the past tense, but that night they would enjoy partying and good beer. Why not? They were on their way to a country that offered them a better way of life.

It took several days before his ship was ready to leave Hamburg, but on the day of his departure, he was not prepared for the size or the crowd going on board. Some were families making the journey with children. Checking everyone's documents was a tedious process that took almost the entire day,

He was ready to begin the final phase of his journey, but as his ship left the dock he turned to take a last look at the land he was leaving forever.

4

An Atlantic Storm

When my father boarded his ship to America, its size helped him feel secure and brought relief to his doubts about sailing across an ocean. The ship was a solid vessel with a seasoned record of crossing the Atlantic, but he was stunned by the number of people heading to steerage.

It was below deck with a large number of cots only two feet apart. He thought of the uncomfortable nights he spent on cots after he left home. He repeated the same experience he did before, but this one was in the middle of a ship with a cot as a bottom bunk and another on top of it. His cousin had settledd in the stern of the ship drinking liquor.

His first problem was with the food. He was served herring at an early meal that tasted as bad as it smelled. He did not get sea sick from it, but he was not able to eat for several days. He was given stale white bread, but he hated it. Only his mother's dark bread helped sustain him, while it lasted. A kitchen helper gave him hot water for his tea. He lost more than ten pounds on the voyage, but only sips of his father's liquor kept him from losing more weight. The liquor energized him, but he yearned for a home cooked meal.

The crowding in steerage was a bigger issue. With no portholes to let in fresh air conditions became unbearable. At times, he rushed on deck to escape the stifling feeling of claustrophobia. There was also a shortage of fresh water that troubled him. It was in short supply that made it difficult to follow his mother's instruction to wash every day.

He found a way to overcome the problem using cold sea water pumped aboard the ship. The bad food and the lack of fresh water were enough to remind him of his early objections to cross an ocean.

The voyage started as a relaxing experience, but the ship soon reached the ocean where it encountered a storm. Instead of plunging ahead, the ship's speed was reduced to wait for the storm to subside, but it continued to grow in strength and intensity. When huge ocean waves hit the ship, it rocked like a toy in a bathtub that left the passengers concerned. Many feared it might endanger the children, who were often crying that added to everyone's fears

A storm on the Atlantic Ocean is nothing new going to and from Europe, but it was an experience my father would have gladly passed. Crewmen said the next day the weather conditions would get worse. They were right with both their timing and prediction.

The following morning the storm cut a wide path, and the ship was caught in the middle of it, as ocean waves crashed over the deck with a fearful force. A storm at sea is always dangerous, but the passengers hoped the ship was strong enough to withstand the battering, as it plunged up and down against the pounding force of the waves. After several days of slow progress, the storm subsided to everyone's relief in steerage. They had been penned up without fresh air.

An estimated number of immigrants came to America in 1905, an astounding number that was only the beginning. On many days, five to six thousand were processed at Ellis Island, the chief U.S. immigration entry point from Europe, according to authorities.

Most immigrants had dramatic stories to tell of their crossing the Atlantic Ocean in steerage with bad food and storms. The most difficult problem for my father was his not being able to speak English.

Historians see their reports as part of the overall adventure new arrivals encountered on their journey. Many Americans can trace their ancestry to those young, enterprising men and women, who from 1880 to 1924 made the voyage to America. Some came earlier and others later, but they all had an episode to relate.

5

Arrival

His ship reached New York early in the morning. Actually, it arrived the night before, but it lingered outside the harbor until the next morning to coincide with the work schedule at Ellis Island.

At daybreak, my father went on deck that was already crowded with immigrants getting their first glimpse of their new country. His friend, who shared the trek with the horse and wagon expressed his relief to be in America.

"We made it across the ocean," he said.

"Thanks God," my father replied.

He felt secure for the first time since the start of a voyage that was full of distress, but now his concern left him. Many passengers were crowding the deck, crying with delight over the sight of the city, but he only smiled as he looked at the scene.

He remembered the translator in Hamburg said seeing New York for the first time was an exciting experience, especially the Statue of Liberty. It was a dramatic symbol impossible to take for granted. It inspired him without knowing why. He liked the Statue's appearance, but was surprised to learn it was a gift from France.

He thought its massive size represented strength, as much as it did liberty, despite being a statue of a woman. The time had arrived to board a barge to take him across the river to an area that is now Battery Park, where immigrants were interrogated and issued a new ID tag. It hung from his jacket as a quick means of identification that coincided with his name on the ship's manifest.

He began to feel proud and thought of the tag as a kind of a positive symbol. It made him feel proud and strong. He was ushered onto a small boat that brought him to Ellis Island and stepped ashore propelled by the force of the jubilant immigrants. They pressed forward toward the main building to complete the final process of their entry to America.

His pace quickened with expectation and felt the excitement to keep up with the crowd, as it hurried to the entry area. He had his small bag, which was much less than anyone else carried. It contained all his worldly goods that included the new shoes his father gave him and the bottle of liquor that helped ease his ocean crossing, except it was now empty.

He was assured it would be easy to fill.

It would be a busy day on Ellis Island. A shipload of passengers was in front of him and two more behind. He kept clapping in support of his good fortune. Why not, he said. He had crossed an ocean.

NEWYORKFERRIESIN1905

Skyline of New York City from New Jersey.

The New York skyline in 1905 when my father arrived
in America. It was a favourite day for him to go from
Jersey City for the pleasure of being on a calm water.
Picture is with shown with thepermissin the the
permission of Jersey City's Main Public Library.

He could not believe so many immigrants were coming to America. Their impact was like the waves over the bow of the ship during the storm he endured, except they represented a more positive impression. He was glad to be a part of it, and his new confidence grew from the euphoria he felt, but could not explain. It was similar to the same feelings he had after his first glimpse of the Statue Liberty on the Hudson River. All he knew was that he was excited. The lines formed at the building entrance were difficult, but he was patient. He knew it would clear for him. He would soon be in America with his sister, who would sign the approval form for his entry. He hoped his final processing would not be long, but he said his reaching the interviewer would take almost the entire day. As he moved forward, his ID tag was checked several times, which was a common practice to observe new arrivals for a physical illness, but he had no medical problems.

In twenty years, the policy that initiated the mass migration to America would be halted by official edict, but not on this day, as the crowd attested. Finally, my father was led upstairs, where immigrants were being interviewed before their entry was completed.

He was awed by the enormous size called the Great Hall. The name was an apt description of the area that was at least a three story auditorium with a walkway near the top. Large arched windows filled the room with sunlight, giving it a positive aura. It was originally without seating, but now there were long rows of benches that were set up around the area like a maze. He felt they helped ease the tension the process generated, but he was glad it would be his final interview, as he waited with others to be called. The immigrants created another problem. Their constant din from conversations echoed off the tiled walls, adding to the difficulty of hearing what anyone said.

The process took longer than he imagined. He told his friends it might take as long to reach the interviewer, as it did to cross the ocean. They laughed over his bland humor was the only joke he told during the entire voyage. It seemed to confirm the release of his pent up emotions because they kept laughing.

Finally, he was called to be interviewed. There were many reports of delays in the processing, but were mostly about trivial matters compared to the vast number that passed through the system on a daily basis. It was an anxious time for immigrants, who were glad when the final process was completed and their admission approved. He was no exception.

It took more than a half day before he was called by the interviewer, but the realization that it was his final interview excited him. His cousin was at his side, but he hoped he would remain quiet. His recollection was that the interviewer was patient as well as friendly, which helped ease his tension, as the translator relayed a series of questions and his responses were noted by the interviewer.

"Where are you from?"

"I'm a Rusyn from Austria," he answered.

The translator explained his Rusyn heritage, but the interviewer wrote Austria on his admission form. He nodded his understanding of Rusyn history and continued the interview.

"Where are you going to live?"

"Pennsylvania."

"How are you going to get there?"

"My sister will take me."

"Is she coming for you?"

"Yes," he replied.

"Do you have any money?"

"She's bringing it."

No question was asked about a job, a usual query for new immigrants, but it was probably omitted on purpose because of his age. After checking his papers, the interviewer said everything was approved, but his sister had not arrived to sign his admission form and he would not be allowed entry until she did. He was confused, but there was no way for him to contact her. He was detained, but could go to New York with his cousin, which he refused to do. He was close to entering his new country, but the negative turn of events depressed him.

Where was she, he wondered?

What he didn't know was that she was staying in Jersey City, a short boat ride away and had come to Ellis Island the day before. If his ship had not been held outside the harbor his ferry to the mainland would have been completed. He thought about his near rejection during his interview in Hamburg, but that experience was much easier for him to accept.

He wanted to laugh, but he felt no humor over his latest hurdle. It was another challenge he had to face, but for the first time he did not feel free, even though he was in a country of enormous freedom.

"America, where are you," he asked?

He was annoyed to be detained after his long journey. It did not take long for him to be in despair. He needed his sister, but it upset him to think he had to rely on her to attain his entry. He was only a boy, but he was certain he would prove his value to his new country, except he felt he was a victim of a system he could not understand.

America wanted him and he wanted America. He had crossed an ocean to prove it, but now he had to deal with his sister signing his entry papers. Why? What did it matter? Could she work in a coal mine? His nerves were wearing thin, but his negative thoughts were interrupted.

"C'mon," an official said.

He did not understand the order, except the tug on his arm was the only signal he needed to follow the direction, as he had done ever since he arrived. No more than two hours had passed since his interview, but it seemed longer. The translator said his sister had arrived and signed his entry form. He was exhilarated to learn his brief detention was over and went to meet her. She was in the reception area and his heart raced with a positive feeling.

Her name was Justina. She was five years older than him and the link to his coming to America. She had encouraged him to make the journey, despite his age, through letters she wrote to their local priest in their homeland. She had arrived in America several years before and settled in Pennsylvania, where she arranged for my father to work in a coal mine with a countryman. It was the plan his father had for him that was nearing fulfilment.

Seeing her filled him with hope. He was grateful he had survived the storm. His emotions could be heard with sounds of joy and a feeling that made him want to dance. Mostly, he was glad to leave his fears behind him, and when the small boat he rode from Ellis Island reached Jersey City, he jumped up and down to be sure he was not dreaming, as his sister laughed at his antics. He felt his long journey was over, not realizing it was just beginning.

6

New Friends

It was always convenient for New York workers to commute from Jersey City by subway or a ferry boat across the Hudson River. The goal was not achieved at the level it has now until the development of office buildings and condominiums were erected on the waterfront If you know the area, it's hard to imagine the change, but to see the development is a stunning experience.

No one ever imagined a major renovation, certainly not immigrants or even existing citizens of the city. The scene my father saw when he arrived in America was an impressive sight, but the scene was not in Jersey City it was in New York. Actually, immigrants were not interested in waterfront developments in the 1900's. They had a more urgent need to get a steady job, but also wanted to celebrate their good fortune to be in America. After he arrived, my father was spending time partying the time away with new friends, as his sister planned for him. She wanted him to relax after his journey. A significant immigrant population had been established in Jersey City and he was now one of them. It was no trouble to be accepted to such an informal group that had left the old country for a new one. Many of the men he met were Rusyns who were twenty years old, but despite the fact that he looked younger he said he was seventeen, cheating on his age.

Some members of the clan were working, while others were still looking for a job. There was always a steady opportunity for low paid immigrants to do simple work that made them a primary source for quick jobs. A motto immigrants liked was to eat a good meal to be ready to work tomorrow. My father laughed, but followed it. He was glad to have time to eat stuffed cabbage and sing the nights away with songs of his homeland with new friends. Going to work in a coal mine would come later.

He was experiencing a change from one thing he had known to another that challenged him. Everyone seemed to have a positive belief in the future, not like his home land, where people were often filled with foreboding. He was in America and wondered why he ever worried about leaving home except for missing his parents.

New immigrants believed in the opportunities America offered, but they also wanted to enjoy its pleasures. It was easy for him to fit into that plan but there was so much to learn about his new country, especially to speak English.

He also wanted to ride in the new transit called the automobile, except he did not know how to pronounce the word in English, but liked the word car. It sounded forceful, but the autos of the early 1920's were shabby. All he wanted was to know what made them run.

To talk about cars was often a man's discussion, but electric powered trolleys were the most popular means of transportation in cities. My father said he enjoyed riding them, especially when the motormen clanged a bell to alert passengers as the trolley sped around a corner. A trolley line was still operating in the city when I was a boy. I told my father I had as much pleasure riding them as he did.

As a new arrival, he was also pleased to learn about dances at the Ukrainian Hall, as well as ferries to take him across the river to New York to see its sights, but he was warned to be careful. Both cities could be dangerous for a lone immigrant at night, when gangs roamed the streets.

It was the first indication he had of a problem, but what troubled him more were warnings about coal mining. His friends said many immigrants preferred to work in a steel mill that was above ground and paid more, but his sister insisted he would be "fine." She said he would learn about coal mining when he got to Pennsylvania.

A bigger problem would be to learn English. His friends described it as a difficult language. He railed against the word "greenhorn," It was a term used to describe an immigrant as an inexperienced usurper, who wanted to take a job away from a worker. He began to feel America might not be as easy to cope with as he thought, but followed his sister's advice and put aside negative feelings.

My father reminded himself that his brother and sister had established a life in America. He had no need to try to find a job. He already had one at a coal mine. In the meantime, he would enjoy his time in the city. He loved going to bars to drink beer, but his friends were quick to point out that conflicts could occur and the police who came to stop a fracas treated immigrants harshly.

Jersey City had a large Irish population and many policemen were Irish. They were as tough as their reputation and did not tolerate a bar ruckus. Many immigrants had learned to avoid a turmoil at a bar My father thought he was hearing a lot of things he wished he had not learned. In time he would have many Irish friends that made him feel secure.

One day, his sister took him to St. Peter and Paul's Orthodox Church, downtown in the city. She gently pushed him into a pew to urge him to say a prayer. He whispered his family's private petition, which was their plea for happiness. They never prayed for success, but felt they needed help to achieve a happy life. The prayer my father described was a special kind of request.

The Pastor asked if he would see him in church on Sunday, but his sister said they were leaving for Pennsylvania, where he would work in a coal mine. After her response, the Pastor gave my father a hug. He hoped he was not sympathizing with him over what he would go at to work.

An anxiety was building in his mind with the same feeling about coal mining that he had about crossing an ocean. He knew he would have to wait until he got to Pennsylvania to learn what digging coal was like, but he was glad he had said a prayer in church. It enabled him to maintain a positive spirit of a new job and a new life.

7
Coal Mine

My father was on his way to Pennsylvania to be a coal miner. He had his sister with him as a guide and was sure he could not have made the way without her.

They left Jersey City for Philadelphia, where they would change trains for Shenandoah, a coal mining hub in Eastern Pennsylvania. A family friend from a village near his home would meet them with a horse and wagon to take them Mahanoy City. My father would work with him in the mine.

When they left Newark, the scenery was flat and different from his homeland with its mountain views. As the train approached Philadelphia, he thought the city sprawled in all directions and asked his sister about it. She knew nothing about the city's colonial history, except it was where they would change trains.

He followed her as she went to the ticket window in the station. He had to be quick to keep up with her and wondered what made her scurry as fast as she did.

It must be the American way. They made their way to the train, which was not as crowded as it was on his way to Hamburg. They settled in seats opposite each other. It was a warm day and he was glad they were next to an open window. The seats were comfortable, but the smoke from the engine entered the railcar and kept him from taking a nap. Like a seasoned traveler he moved across the aisle to a better seat, but couldn't stop worrying about what was ahead for him.

Less than two weeks had passed since he left Ellis Island, but his whole world had changed. He was no longer in a small rural village in Eastern Europe and only hoped he was suited for the bustling new world. He wished he had stayed in Jersey City longer, except he left with his sister when she said it was time to leave. A month before he left home, he had not been anywhere, but rode a train from Poland to Germany and sailed across an ocean. Now, he was speeding his way into Pennsylvania.

Mixed emotions troubled him, as he compared the "old country" to a new one. He was glad to be in America, but leaving home had not been easy. He felt his journey had enough experiences to fill a lifetime and told his sister about his concerns.

She understood and said everything would soon be good for him when he went to work in the coal mine. He would earn money that would give him the confidence to make him feel like an adult, not a lonely teenager. She reassured him the way his mother did. Her support eased his concern and he felt relaxed. He was tired and napped, despite the smoke from the train's engine.

It was early afternoon when he finally arrived in Shenandoah. Sam Wistyrka a neighbor in Europe, and the miner he would work with was waiting for him. He was years older than my father and worked in the coal mine since coming to America seven years earlier, except my father did not remember him.

They left for Mahanoy City in Sam's horse and wagon. He wanted to show off the area, but first he asked my father to update him on his parents and the journey to America. He was anxious to tell him about the ocean storm he endured, plus the friends he made in Jersey City. He was sure Sam wanted to explain coal mining, but he kept talking about the countryside with its hills that were like their homeland. Sam did not discuss coal mining, which pleased my father.

Sam first wanted to become acquainted.

He was a pixie, a little more than five feet tall, but a skilled miner with a personality that matched his image. He wore high laced boots that almost reached his knees. They made him look like a comic figure, but not when it came to coal mining. He was a top producer, which earned him the respect of his boss, as well as the miners. Mostly, he was easy to like and my father felt confident about working with him.

During his first night, there was a party at the house of one of Sam's friends. It was a carefree time, just as there had been in Jersey City. The next day after

Sunday's church service, Sam took him to meet several coal miners who were Rusyns. They were friendly and asked many questions about the "old country."

That night there was another gathering at Sam's house, but my father said he had enough of partying and wanted to rest. Sam led him upstairs to a bedroom, where he laid on one of the beds. He felt at ease, pushing off his shoes that fell to the floor with a thud, but he ignored them, as he yawned and stretched out his arms full of contentment.

"America is a wonderful country," he said.

"Yes," Sam said.

"My Poppa was right."

"About what," Sam asked.

"America," he responded.

"Wait until tomorrow," Sam stated.

"Why. What happens tomorrow?"

"We go to work in the mine."

"Tomorrow," he asked rising from the bed?

"Yes, but I want you to meet my co-miner."

"At the mine," he asked with concern?

"Yes. Then we will go to see the boss."

"Will there be a job for me?"

"Sure, don't worry. You will work with me."

Telling my father not to worry was like asking the stars not to come out on a clear night. He knew it would be important and could only sleep a short time. He arose at 5:00AM full of anxiety, but Sam had arrived with the wagon ready to take him to the mine. He kept a slow pace to explain how coal mining was done early in the 20th Century, which was different from what it is today.

In addition to miners, who were the backbone of coal mining, he described other areas, including "mule drivers and "buttys," which was what miners' helpers were called. The word sounded peculiar to him, but he would work as Sam's "butty."

America was depended on anthracite coal mined throughout Pennsylvania and Mahanoy City mines. Sam explained that anthracite burned longer and cleaner that produced a long lasting burn and heat than other coals. It was used in many businesses, as well as in homes. At its height, there were 15 or more mines in area of Mahanoy City that mined anthracite coal every work day.

Sam took him through the city, which was more like a town, but he wanted my father to see the lush green hills in the area and the entrance to the mine. What was important, Sam said the coal from mines in Mahanoy City was in great demand that supported a strong community of dedicated mine workers. The entry ways of the mines presented a neat appearance that impressed my father. It was a positive image my father said was not ravaged and thought the mines would be as neat.

Sam was pleased with his response.

He asked Sam about a group of small houses on a nearby hill. He explained they were coal mine owned houses built for the convenience of the miners. The residents called it a comfortable community, but for those who could afford it lived farther away from the mine. His sister was at the edge of town in a small house, but Sam lived far away from the mine, where there was a typical country environment.

It was time for them to meet Phil O'Toole, who was Sam's mining partner and a top producer. Like Sam, he had a calm, confident manner that made it easy for them to work together. Phil O'Toole was not Sam's only mining friend, but he was the best. They worked together, but each with their own helper that proved to be productive arrangement.

Immigrant miners often wanted to partner with someone who was fluent in English to help ease communications with other miners. Obviously, Phil O'Toole was an Irishman with no language problem, but he was also qualified to ignite small explosives to bring down a wall of coal. The combination made him a perfect mining partner.

Sam's previous helper left for another job, but buttys were never missed. Miners were the premiere workers in a coal mine and getting his partner's approval of a helper was only a curtesie. Sam could have any one he wanted to be his helper, but he did not want to offend Phil O'Toole. He was concerned over my father's lack of experience. He told Sam he was not convinced he was ready to work in a coal mine. Sam understood, but remained steadfast, as Phil O'Toole continued to match his negative resolve.

The main responsibility for a helper was to load coal cars as fast as he could to keep the area clear of obstruction for miners to do their work. A miner's earnings were not based on an hourly rate, but on the amount of coal produced.

Counting filled coal cars was an easy way to measure results, and a helper could be a vital member of the team to achieve set goals. Sam remained firm my father would be a top notch helper. He knew his family and said he could do the job. Knowing that Sam was so supportive, Phil O'Toole finally relented and gave up his objection of my father.

"Okay" was all he said.

It was a weak approval, but Sam took my father to meet the boss. If Sam was elfin in size, his boss was not much taller, but a short stature was an asset in low mine areas. His name was Kelly, a tough Irishman, who greeted Sam with a firm handshake. It was a friendly gesture, but a silent contest of arm strength they had engaged in many times before. Finally, they relaxed their grip, laughing over their macho test.

Sam introduced my father to Kelly in English then reversed the order and the language for Kelly to meet my father. He was impressed at how confidently Sam spoke English. He was sure it made it easy for him to be thought of as a coal miner, not just an immigrant worker

He realize how important it was to learn English. He would never forget the meeting. It was the start of his becoming an American citizen.

Every coal mine has a special character and Kelly fit the mold. No one knew his first name or cared, but it didn't take long for him to become a top earning miner. He did it starting as a mule driver, hauling coal from a mine. Sam felt that Kelly would question my father's age and his response would be negative.

Kelly preferred maturity in his miners, including helpers, and spoke of it often. Sam was worried. With his lack of experience, he hoped my father would be able to do the work. He wanted to avoid any discussion about his age, except he felt sure Kelly would challenge him, which led to Sam to add to my father's age.

He said he was seventeen.

"Don't try to fool me," Kelly said. "He's a kid, and you know how I feel about kids in the mine."

"He'll be a good worker," Sam emphasized.

"Let's make him a mule driver," Kelly said.

"No," Sam said. "I want him to be my butty."

"Okay," Kelly replied. "You Rusyns always stick together, but it's your ass, if he doesn't work out."

"Yeah, I know, but you're a bastard," Sam said.

"You can bet on it," Kelly laughed.

Following his boss' remark, Sam told my father about the discussion, but he realized his clumsy effort was a mistake. My father could not understand the problem.

He felt his age had nothing to do with working in the mine. Either he could do the work or not, but pleased when it was settled and the decision approved. He made his mark on several papers before heading to the mine carrying basic tools, including a pick and shovel.

He entered the lift with Sam that would take him down to the mine. It was a deep descent and the change from sunlight to and a dimly lit mine disturbed him, not an unusual reaction. Veteran miners often became disoriented going down a mine shaft.

His first impression was that it was a harsh environment. Mostly, he hated being below ground. The small lantern on the helmet he wore only illuminated a limited area. An odor of damp earth produced a constant chill from water that leaked into the mine. He did not know it, but the water leaks could weaken beams and lead to a cave in that miners feared.

The work started immediately.

There was no time to get use to the job. Sam told him to stay close and load the coal cars with as little rocks as possible, as fast as he could do it. If he was worried before, he felt trapped in a world he never imagined. But he began his career as a coal miner's helper. It required loading the cars quickly. Mining coal was hard work, but loading it was more strenuous. A lot of shovelling and heavy lifting was required to clear the space for the miners to do their work.

Phil O'Toole and his helper were hardly friendly. They nodded a brief hello, so he did the same. It usually took a full day to fill four coal cars, but by noon, over three cars had been loaded. He out did the other helper, but the strenuous labor of lifting a shovel after shovel of coal, as well to remove heavy stones, made him realize it would not be easy. He laughed to think as he ounce did about loading coal and tending his vegetable garden.

But his short trial in the coal mine was over.

At their lunch break, Sam told Phil O'Toole everything about his new helper. He listened with a new respect about this young bantam rooster with the wide chest, huge arms and strong legs. Despite his age, he had contributed more than the other booty filling coal cars. Phil O'Toole apologized for doubting him and called him a coal miner.

He appreciated the compliment, but it did not ease his fears. The first day was all it took for him to realize mining coal was hard work in a dark tunnel. Coal dust covered him, adding to his depressed feeling, but he did not mention it to Sam, who was content with his life as a miner.

He returned to his sister's house a blackened image, glad to be alive and see a large metal tub had been set up in the back yard for him to bathe. The tub was in the middle of a low fence that circled it on three sides. While he was bathing, a neighbour passed on his way to an outhouse, but walked around the tub's fence to talk to him. He did not object to the intrusion. It was not privacy he needed, but a hot bath. His visitor only spoke English, which happily limited their conversation.

On Sundays, he bathed twice, once in the morning and again at night, but he had to chop extra wood to heat water for two baths. They helped ease the strain of his aching body, as well as to wash away the coal dust he hated. Bathing outdoors became a daily ritual, but later, when the weather turned colder, he would wash indoors. Few coal miners' homes had a bathroom with a tub, but the metal basin outside suited him, as long as the water was warm.

A year passed and each day was like the one before. He continued going down in the mine, but wanted to give up coal mining, except he was uncertain of where to go and what he would do. After another two years passed, he was eighteen and had achieved manhood. If he was taken for being older before, he told everyone he was twenty one.

He learned to speak English, but with an accent described as pleasant. He was proud to speak and understand some English. He began to feel acclimated and bragged about being a coal miner. He spent his free time going to local bars, where there were always women chasing a young buck from the mine.

His social activity reviled his loneliness. He did what his mother wanted him to do. He went to church to hear the liturgy. Later he would hum the sacred vocals. His friends thought he was religious, but the chants reminded him of his home.

Life was a series of digging coal and scrubbing baths for a Saturday night party and Sunday church. Without knowing what the term meant, he was in a rut working in a dark mine. It was a Saturday night at a local bar and he spoke with the bartender. He earned less than he expected.

"No one got rich digging coal."

"I know," he said." it's killing me."

"Yeah sure," the bartender said.

"You'll see. I'm quitting."

"Good luck," the bartend added.

"You'll need it."

8

A New Start

In 1908 my father took the same train to Philadelphia he rode three years before, except he was alone now and on his way in a reverse direction back to Jersey City not to a coal mine.

When he left the city three years before, he had his sister with him and a job. Now, he was on his own, doing what he wanted to do, but without a job and no one to advise him. He felt a barrier had been lifted when he left the coal mine, but he learned several things about himself. One was that a steady job often insured security. The other was that he hated to be alone and always made friends on a job.

Neither reaction was unique, but if leaving home was a challenge, finding a job in a city could be more difficult It required knowing how read and write, except his needs were not extreme. All he wanted was to earn enough money to live on, "plus a little left over." He did not think about building a nest egg. No unskilled immigrant planned that far ahead, but he had a more immediate goal. He wanted to find a job he liked.

It was the extent of his American dream. He had learned to speak English that he felt increased his job value, but it was a short sighted appraisal. To read and write, as well as to speak English would have added to his income. After three years, he adapted to new customs, but still had a lot to learn about America. If he was a farm boy, he would have had hayseed in his hair, but he lost the hayseed in a coal mine. He was no longer a "country bumpkin" or "Greenhorn," except he did not realize new struggles were ahead as the conductor brought him back to reality.

"Philadelphia," he announced.

"Phil-del-fi-a," he repeated, dropping the first "a" in its name his accent forced him to do. Listen to me Poppa, he thought, I can speak English. He waited to change trains and remembered the phrase about Philadelphia being: "The City of Brotherly Love." He laughed over his new found knowledge, pleased with himself as he waited for his train.

He stood waiting to leave and wondered if the passengers could ride a wagon through Poland. It was a silent challenge, but it made him smile. He didn't think of himself as an immigrant foreigner any more, but as an American. He liked the feeling and thought he could go anywhere a train could take him. Maybe he would go "West" and become a cowboy. Coal miners often talked about them. He thought it was fun to fantasize, something he could never do before.

A Busy Street in the 1900's

Newark Avenue in Jersey City near my father
lived after returning to the city.
Early 1900'sPicture appears with the permission
of Jersey City's Main Public Library.

He was no longer homesick, except his feelings about his parents remained with him. He had forgotten about the bed that once had been so important to him, but it was Sunday, a busy day for all he had to do. First, he went to church, as he had promised the priest. Then he went to see his mining partner, Sam, who was not happy he was leaving. It caused Sam to stumble over his parting words not knowing what to say.

He wore a new pea coat and cap, but the cap was a gift from Sam. It was genuine Irish tweed. He was certain it had cost at least a dollar or maybe as much as two dollars. He was moved by the gift and gave Sam a hug, then quickly withdrew.

He remembered the priest in Jersey City hugged him before he left for the coal mine, which made him feel awkward, as it did hugging Sam. They had been through a lot together, sharing a special intimacy in a dark mine. Now, he was breaking their bond, but they would not speak of it. There was no easy way to say goodbye, but my father did it in a classic manner with a flick of his cap.

A survey indicated that life expectancy in 1900 was only forty seven years for men, a troubling statistic that confirmed a short, hard life. Medical drugs were in the future. At the same time, a change occurred that brought a new level of economic growth to the nation.

The auto industry was becoming a major factor creating jobs. In another decade historians would claim it had a dramatic impact on the economy. There were many problems with automobiles, some did not stop anyone from driving, despite the often heard calls "to get a horse" when a car broke down.

By 1908, there were 8,000 automobiles on the road in America. A car was the most important item to own, except for a house, but less than 200 miles of roads were paved outside a city. A speed limit of 20 miles per hour was also posted in twenty states, but 10 miles per hour was the speed limit within most towns to minimize reckless driving.

The assembly line would revolutionize manufacturing in the auto industry. In 1913 it enabled Ford to cut the time to produce a Model-T car that reduced its cost and sale price, making it the most popular car in America. Henry Ford doubled the wage of assembly line workers from $2.50 per day to $5.00. It was a dramatic change in their pay scale, but many claimed Ford took advantage of assemble line workers by threatening them to keep up or lose a pay increase that enabled his workers to buy a new Ford car.

By mid-decade, American industry was in an expanding mood with advances in technology and entertainment products, such as record players. People sang songs aloud after listening to hits "Sweet Adeline" on a hand cranked RCA Victrola record player. However, my father was more concerned over someone named Carrie Nation, who was on a personal crusade against the consumption of liquor, swinging her infamous axe in bars to stop their sale. He worried where the nation was headed.

Five years before the Wright brothers had flown in an "aero plane." My father could hardly believe it, but flying had become the nation's new phenomenon. In sports, baseball was America's most popular game. The Chicago Cubs beat the Detroit Tigers in the 1908 World Series, but he watched my brother Paul play football and my father became a fan of the game.

The city was thriving as immigrants continued to arrive, but there were more references to the word "Greenhorn" than before. He ignored it. The cost for everything increased, mostly for rents, except odd jobs kept him from worrying about his meals. If he was hungry would eat a sandwich at a bar from a spread of cold cuts included with a shot of liquor and a beer chaser for a dime, plus a nickel tip.

He saved money from his coal mining pay, but events took a bad turn. After sending money home and paying a week's rent, he had $35 left of his savings. Early in the afternoon, he was in his room with several other immigrants waiting for cleaners to do the work was in demand from all the residents equally to ease the pay;

His bag was larger now, but he toted it easily. Before going out, he took $2 from an envelope, except he made the mistake of exposing his cash. When he returned the money was gone.. He searched for it, but knew he had been robbed. It left him destitute. He was disappointed over the casual way to protect his savings, but the money he saved from the coal mine was gone. He was deeply hurt at first then angry.

Another resident insisted he get the police, but he felt no one could help him recover his money, except a short time later a local policeman entered the scene. Appropriately, he was a tall, confident Irishman named Casey, who went about his investigation in a methodical way. His authoritative tone quieted his anxiety, but he could not ease his remorse.

When he described the detail to the policeman, he felt returning to the city may have been a wrong decision. He was sure none of his money would be recovered, even if the thieves were caught, but the policeman said you can never be sure, except he was critical of my father's carelessness.

"Do you think you can catch the crooks?"

"Don't worry. I'll get them," he stated.

"I hope so," my father said.

"That was a lot of money to leave in a bag."

"Yes," he answered with regret.

"I know you wanted your friends to see how good you did digging for gold" the policeman added.

"Digging for coal," he said annoyed.

"I meant for coal," Casey snickered.

My father thought it was a sarcastic attempt to embarrass him. He knew he should not have taken the money from his envelope for everyone to see. His first experience on his own had been a disaster. He was depressed and ridiculed by a policeman, who bragged he would catch the crooks.

He almost laughed, except he wanted to cry.

"Let's go," the policeman said abruptly.

"Go? Go where?"

"Just follow me," the policeman said.

He obeyed the command, but wondered where he was taking him. They walked at a slow pace to a small bar, where two men he never saw before huddled at a corner table. After talking to the bartender, the policeman was sure they were the men who had stolen the money. Casey soon arrested them and they confessed. A call was made for a police wagon to take the culprits away. His pay envelope was retrieved and there was $30 in it.

He was ecstatic over the quick action by Casey, who he now called by his name. He knew his "beat" and was sure the thieves had not gone far. They were headed for a bar, where they were not known and could not be identified. Casey felt if he found them before too much time elapsed they would have most of the money.

My father could not have been more elated and wanted to give Casey a reward, but he refused the offer, except they agreed to meet to have a beer to celebrate. Casey said he knew a bar where chicken wings were served with an order for two beers without checking ID's to confirm a costumer's age.

He said smiled over Casey's remark

Recovering his stolen money was the extent of his good luck. An employment search would not be as successful. He was ready to do any kind of work, but the low pay for temporary jobs never satisfied him. Th Over the next year, he had two jobs. In one stint, he worked for a railroad installing rails. The other was on a state project digging a culvert for a water drain.

The low pay didn't help, but he had no recourse. He thought of how much more he earned working in the coal mine. Only skilled workers such as longshoremen, steel workers and construction men earned more, but those jobs were hard to get.

It was not long before his savings were depleted and he was back where he started, without money and unsure of what he would do next. He was relieved to be free of the coal mine, but he had to find his way in the city, as many immigrants had to do before him. The thought was a mental stretch for support, but not as helpful as his bed once was for him. He knew it was a serious time.

All he needed was a job.

9

Anna

My mother's name was Anna.

She lived on the north side of the Carpathian Mountains in a village that was twelve miles from my father's home. It was more than a stone's throw, but closer than the three thousand miles it took for them to meet in America.

Her childhood was a happy one, but she remained motivated by the same urgings of a better life that brought many immigrants to the "new country." She was committed to America for what the "old country" could not give her, except she would say it included meeting an eligible man that made my father laugh.

Many men who migrated to America had the same pursuit to meet a woman he would marry, as my mother said she felt to find her man. The comparison doesn't stop there. A women's need to find a job was the same as it was for an immigrant male. It could be a more difficult than acquiring a potential mate.

My mother said it was worth it.

She sailed to America in 1906 a year after my father from Bremerhaven, Germany. His crossing was on a stormy sea, but no problem. It was a safe voyage and uneventful. Unlike my father, the discomforts in steerage did not disturb her. She was not tired from the journey. It only took the average time four to five days for her crossing, but my father could never forget the storm he encountered doubled the time to reach America.

Her journey was made with an adult aunt and several cousins. She never lost the conviction that her going to America was the right thing for her to do. She had a minimal education, but knew enough English to add to her positive feelings. Several relatives in the city provided her with a place to live, which eased her main concern.

Slight and trim, her lips were always parted in a ready smile that revealed her happy disposition, as if nothing disturbed her. Similar to all the women from her homeland, she was an accomplished cook, but said it was only a minor talent. She was energetic with a positive spirit and often wore a "babushka" or kerchief that covered her head when it was cold. It framed her face and made her smile stand out like a poster of an immigrant girl that promoted coming to America.

Unlike the early pioneers, she never rode a covered wagon, but her inner strength was unmatched. With her determination, she could have driven across the Rockies in a wagon to help lead the nation's expansion. She was not shy, but a product of her time with no strong political beliefs, especially when it came to a woman's place in society. She was a home maker with an independent spirit.

As the transfer boat brought her to Ellis Island, she was filled with enthusiasm and moved with a pace that reflected her upbeat nature. She was anxious to begin her new life, forcing her companions to keep up with her. She made her way forward with a pleasant mood that pleased officials, as they scanned arrivals looking for physical handicaps, except she was not delayed for any medical problem that would have denied her entry.

At the Great Hall, she said others were nervous, but being close to her destination weaving her way through the labyrinth of aisles and benches did not trouble her. She was exuberant and ready to move ahead. Finally, she was called to be interviewed, but when she turned to pick up her cloth bag it caused her to go to the wrong desk.

The translator was perturbed, but the interview official of immigrants laughed over her move, enjoying the momentary break in a busy day. Her carefree attitude showed in her calm approach, as the official asked the interpreter her name.

"Anna Korba," she stated with an accent.

"Oh, you speak English," he said surprised.

"I speak it a little," she replied, with an accent.

"Good," he said.

"I'm ready to be an American?"

"I'm glad. Where are you from?"

"I'm a Rusyn from Austria," she responded.

The interviewer was impressed as the translator stated her background. He said she was a part of an ethnic enclave in Eastern Europe under Austrian control, but the interviewer waved him away with a quick move of his hand. Several thousand Rusyns had immigrated to America through Ellis Island over the previous decade that listed Austria as a part of their country. Officials were familiar with Rusyns' ethnic history.

After a lengthy series of questions, her entry was approved and she moved ahead smiling. She almost clicked her heels in a dance step. Her Aunt arrived and signed her entry form. She was ready to go with her to a new abode in an immigrant area of Jersey City near the waterfront close to where my father lived.

She was quick to look for a job to pay for the prime essentials of rent and food. It was not an easy time for female immigrants, with few jobs for women, and the pay was less than what she sought. Her ability to speak a bit of English didn't help, but she insisted that being in America improved her life over the harsh existence of the "old country." It was not easy to get started without a job. My father agreed, but as a joke someone added except if she went to work in a coal mine.

Several of the jobs she had included one as a seamstress at a crowded New York loft in a dress factory. The pay was based on the number of dresses she sewed. For a time, she also rolled tobacco leaves into a popular cigar brand. She would work at any job to earn the money she needed, including after hours cleaner of business offices.

Immigrants, both men and women, quickly learned to work hard, which was more than a slogan. It was the path to a better future. She was determined, but like most young women she wanted to find a man to and have a family.

For many immigrants, both male and female, it was an important goal, but she believed the right someone would come along. She said she would know, if it was the right choice, as soon as he said "hello." At times laughing over her cherished feelings, she was quick to emphasize my father was her one and only. He would reply in the same way, but added it was too late for her to change her mind.

He said "She was stuck with him," he said.

10

The Meeting

My mother and father could have met in their homeland, but they came to America and fate played its part. They were in Jersey City at a friend's wedding reception, enjoying the festive evening. It was a perfect setting to start a courtship.

The weather was cold and brisk outside with snow on the ground, but inside the reception hall it was heated and warm. My father was perspiring from dancing, but ignored the need to be neat. He loosened his tie and unbuttoned his shirt collar, as he wiped the sweat from his forehead and went to introduce himself to my future mother.

She understood his discomfort and agreed that it was hot inside the hall. After an exchange of names, she realized they knew each other's families from their homeland. It made it easy for them to reminisce, except the orchestra began playing music with a fast beat. My father took advantage of the moment to ask her to dance. It was more than a casual invitation.

He felt that dancing was an uncomplicated way to win a mate, but his first dance with my mother would not be cheek to cheek to a slow ballad, but a fast Polka. He loved the dance with its swift turns, foot stomps and loud shouts that gives the Polka its character. She was not sure she could keep up with him, but tried as he led her around the floor. Their quiet time would come later, but the Polka was the start of their mating ritual. She loved the dance, but was glad to have survived it. He laughed.

It was a time in America when everything was simple. Life was simple and so was falling in love. Quick decisions to wed were a common occurrence, not only for immigrants. His feelings were the same as my mother's. He was certain he would know the woman he wanted as his mate as soon as they met.

My mother was the one.

He was tired of sharing a room with other men and seldom knew them. It was only a room for sleeping and was unattended for days. Clothes were usually scattered about the bed rooms. What was worse, he was the only one who disliked it. It created an unsightly scene he hated, but it was a common experience for immigrant bachelors.

My father needed a change.

My mother said she was ready.

Many immigrant marriages were made because of economic necessity, but he felt they would be happier together than apart. Their commitment was all they needed. It's the usual conviction that always leads to marriage.

He gave her no engagement ring, but they did not wait long to wed. Later, the economic Depression and my mother's illness would plague them, but the start of their lives together would be full of promise.

Their wedding was held at St. Peter and Paul's Russian Orthodox Church on Grand Street at the same church they went to before he left for the coal mine in Pennsylvania. The church has a sturdy presence with an old world charm that augments its religious aura. The day was overcast, but weddings are always a joyous occasions. If there was a good omen it was the rays of sunshine that broke through an overcast sky to add a pleasant glow to the day.

Prior to the ceremony, my father said he was nervous. Not to be outdone, my mother said she felt the same. She wore a white dress, while he was in a navy blue suit and white shirt with a blue tie. Everyone was impressed, but she had bought a purple tie for him that he forgot to wear.

A friend made a round trip and brought the tie to the church. My mother waited patiently, as my father switched ties. The groom usually is the one the bride keeps waiting, but this wedding was a reversal. When he was ready, he nodded to the priest and my mother came down the aisle, holding a small bouquet of red tea roses. He greeted her with a smile and she did the same, pleased he was wearing the purple tie.

"Do you Peter take Anna to be your wife?"

"Do you Anna take Peter as your husband? My mother, who was twenty years old and my father who was twenty-one made their "wedding vows." Everyone thought they were right for each other. It was a simple ceremony, but he said he heard birds sing and bells ring. He had never been so clever with words before. They were only a bit of verbal humor my mother said she heard, too.

She was a homebody who loved domestic things, while my father was primed to party. A quiet wedding suited her, but the party that followed was loud and full of the fun he wanted. The reception was at the Ukrainian Hall, where they met. It was near to closing at 1:PM, but many guests continued partying. There were more than 60 revellers at the event. Some my parents did not know. My father only urged them to have a good time. Among his friends, wedding receptions were judged by the amount of whiskey consumed and the polkas danced. My father saw to it that his wedding reception would be one of the best with the amount of drinks served and the polkas danced. I never knew where he got money. It was probably a chip in the guests made. It didn't matter. My mother was amazed at his energy. He always wanted to dance and urged my mother to dance, but she feared he meant the Polka. Her "Petrush," as she called him would party all night, but he did not object when she wanted to leave.

"I'm ready "Anyce," he said, using his endearment for Anna he called my mother.

Their married lives together began in furnished downtown rooms in Jersey City, close to Bright Street. My father said the rooms were small, but included a kitchen, bedroom and front room with a worn two seat sofa and straight back chair. The only problem was the bathroom was shared by two tenants It was a common arrangement, but it did have a low cost arrangement and a bathtub.

The rent was $10 dollars a month.

11

Lessons to Learn

My Father's skills were limited to the strength of his forearms and energy that enabled him to do any kind of labor. It was the basis of his confidence, but there were few jobs, a petty report by now.

He had no knowledge of the industrial developments that were changing America. They demanded more from its workers, so much more. His most important need had been to learn to read and write English, except he felt he had to work to live. He could not let anything interfere with that purpose. It came out first. Learning to read and write English would come later he said, but it never did.

A program to teach immigrants English was not available, as it is today. It took him three years to learn to speak English, but he did it the hard way as he struggled to grasp each word, listening to it over and over until it was etched in his mind. It helped him to read some signs, but not enough. At first, he mispronounced some words with his accent, but he was a good listener and had a friendly manner that provided him with patience. It was a quality he never lost.

His problem remained the same. He could not read or write, and had to make an "X" in place of his name. My mother would teach him to write his name, but it was not enough. He wrote each letter slowly with a deliberate effort that made him feel proud. John said he would admire writing his name, pleased with the result, except it was not enough. He should have continued the process and learned to write more than his name, but he had no one to help him.

His failure is easy to explain.

Many peasants faced the same need to survive in Eastern Europe. His parents needed his youth and strength to sustain their home and grow vegetables. They felt an elementary education was not essential and often not available in the 19th Century and early into the 20th Century. It was a way for poor households in areas of the Carpathian Mountains in Eastern Europe, as well as in poor rural areas of America.

He should have mastered to read and write in his own language, which would have made it easier for him to learn the basics of English that everyone said was difficult. When he arrived in America he had the energy to do it, but he was over whelmed working in a coal mine. After he married my mother and had a family, he felt he had more pressing responsibilities than to learn to read and write English. It was a bold decision, but easier to solve the problem today.

My parents married three years after my father returned to Jersey City from the coal mine. Their courtship was brief, but being together was right for them, too. First, my brother John was born. Then Mike arrived a year later. With two boys, life was full for them. My mother was proud to be the bearer of two sons, but hoped her next child would be a girl.

After another four years, a third boy arrived they named Paul. Pete was born seven years later, and I came five years after his birth. My mother had five sons without the girl she always wanted. My brothers told me many people came to celebrate my christening, but my mother said the party was only an excuse for my father to dance.

You know by now my father loved to do the polka. With their similar backgrounds, they shared a common history and she understood his feelings of nostalgia when it came to dancing. She would soothe him with recollections of their homeland to keep its memories alive. In a way, she wanted to do it for herself, but she filled the role of an amateur psychologist. She told him things would be good for them, adding if he had not left home when he did they would never have met.

When he returned to the city, he felt he was his own man. He was ready to find his way, except he missed the more than $12 dollars a week he made in the coal mine. He couldn't equal that pay, but leaving the mine changed his life. The way he described it, he eluded a tragedy, but he did not know which was worse, hating coal mining or fearing it. He could never feel one emotion without the other, except it wasn't long before he was in need of a job.

After some searching, he went to work in the city on the waterfront at a Sugarhouse for a small wage, but it proved to be a recuperative experience. Molasses and sugarcane were brought in from Cuba to be processed into sugar. He did general maintenance at the plant, as well as working outdoors unloading cargo. It was a strenuous task, but he was overjoyed to be in the fresh air, where he sang songs of his homeland to express his good feelings.

It wasn't long before his friends reacted to his singing and added an appellation to his name. They called him, "Sugarhouse Pete," the guy who sang at work. The name fit his jovial personality, but at home we call him Pop and my mother Mom.

12

A Job and a Fire

In 1910, long before I was born, Jersey City had grown in population to a quarter million with predictions it would reach a million by the end of the century. It never did, despite an immigrant population that had increased to 70,000, nearly one third the city's total. Plans were completed for the construction of the Holland Tunnel that would add impetus to the city's development and promote a new motto: "The City with Everything for Industry."

The list of major firms was impressive and jobs were plentiful, except the pay for labourers remained inadequate, despite the expanding economy. The Colgate Company had a plant on the waterfront near the Sugarhouse to make soap products. The largest outdoor clock in America was on the roof of the Colgate Company that could easily be read across the river in New York that made it a popular landmark.

The American Can Company was busy making cans for a number of products, while the Dixon Pencil plant was creating the country's most popular writing instrument for schools and in business. The Emerson Company had a plant that made radios. Before the health hazard of smoking was known the Lorillard Company was producing a popular cigarette brand in the city called "Kools," but the largest employer was the Pennsylvania Railroad.

Despite the prospects, my mother said my father was still having a problem finding a job he liked. It was not long after he left the coal mine, but he was learning what it meant to be unskilled in America. Most immigrants felt that to get a special job was not practical. It was beyond ordinary yearning. They had little choice than to take any job they could get, but my father remained steadfast searching for a job he would like that was above ground.

One day, his luck changed.

He met Jim Murphy, a friend at a bar he frequented. It was 1914 shortly before the outbreak of World War I. He was preparing to return to Ireland, despite political problems. He was engaged to an Irish girl and their dream was to return home where he would be a farmer.

With the impetus of the automobile, gasoline had become an important product, and Jim Murphy arranged for my father to replace him as a boilermaker or metal worker at a Standard Oil Company refinery. It ultimately located in Linden in sight of the New Jersey Turnpike.

White Horse Wagon
and Derby Hats

Jersey City at Newark Avenue and Erie Streets
in the early 1900's, near where my mother and
father lived after their marriage. Picture is with the
permission of Jersey City's Main Public Library.

The job involved cutting steel plates to repair oil storage tanks to be riveted together. What gave him satisfaction was erecting new tanks. Despite the lack of formal training, he had a facility for metal work. It was the job he always wanted and worked for the company for 41 years.

With the outbreak of World War I the need for oil soared and the economy boomed. Many people hoped America would stay out of the conflict, but it joined the Allies in 1917 for the final, but brutal phase of the conflict. My father was glad not to be in Europe with its centuries old problems over borders and a series of petty conflicts.

My parents had two young sons and in 1916 when my mother gave birth to my brother Paul to make it three. A catastrophe struck that year that caused more anguish than they had known. It was a Saturday night in October when my father helped a friend move, which delayed his returning home. In the evening a fire broke out in our rooms. John was five, Mike four and Paul little more than several months old. John smelled fumes from the hallway and went to warn my mother. At first, she paid no attention, but he returned to tell her the hall was full of smoke.

There was nothing more threatening in the city than a tenement fire. One look at the smoke seeping under the door made her respond quickly. With her new baby and my other brothers, she led the way down a back fire escape to safety before the fire engulfed her rooms on the second floor. She escaped without concern for anything except her children, but regretted not having the time to save her wedding pictures, as well as a few family photographs. Once safely out of the tenement she told a fireman she would be staying with a neighbour across the street.

The fire started on the first floor when a resident dropped a kerosene lamp. It did not take long for it to be out of control. Every tenant made it out safely, but a family on the third floor, including a mother and two young children were taken to the hospital as a precaution to relieve smoke inhalation. They were scheduled to be released the next morning, which was a positive report. When my father reached his tenement, enough time had elapsed to create a chaotic scene. The fire was contained, but smoke was still filtering from the building. Fire engines were blocking the street and there were firemen moving in every direction. After observing the scene, my father was concerned over what may have happened to his family He asked several onlookers if they had seen my mother. One observer said she had been caught in the fire with his children. That report frightened him. A nearby fireman heard the comment and went to question him.

"You're the man's family caught in the fire?"

"Yes," he said to contain himself.

A little clarity would have eliminated the problem. The fireman should have said that nothing serious happened to any tenant, but my father's response didn't help. His troubled emotions did not allow him to sort out the mishap. He blamed himself for what he thought was a tragedy that could have been avoided, if he had gotten home at his usual time.

Mostly, he did not grasp the innocent instruction to go to the hospital. He thought he would have to identify his family's remains, which was a gruesome prospect. The fireman could have eased his anguish, but tragedy often causes the distortion of simple facts.

This fire was no exception.

Of course, in hindsight it should have been easy to resolve. A simple explanation would have avoided the mix up and spared any distress, but the fireman was anxious to attend to other duties. My father was glad to see him go. He had become too distraught to listen to anything the fireman said.

He stayed up all night with friends who kept offering him liquor, but he couldn't drink. In the morning, still overcome with grief, he went to view the scene before going to the hospital. A neighbour saw him and casually said how wonderful it was for his wife and children to be saved, especially his new baby. He couldn't believe what she said.

"My family was saved," he asked stunned?

"Yes," his neighbour said enthusiastically.

"What," he repeated unsure of what she said.

"They were so lucky," she said.

"My wife and boys are okay?"

"Yes, didn't anyone tell you"?

"No, I thought they were caught in the fire."

"They're fine," she repeated.

He expressed his gratitude and raced across the street to where my mother and brothers spent the night. He was wiped out of all his material possessions. His emotions went from deep despair to grateful euphoria then back to lingering concern. He was penniless without a place to live and lied to himself, so he could lie to my mother.

"Everything will be all right," he told her. Their church and friends in the community were the most help, but my mother never failed to praise John as a hero who saved the family.

The Lady in Command

Jersey City waterfront development in the
background of the Statue of Liberty.
The picture appears with the permission of the
Jersey City Development Corporation.

My parents found rooms on Sussex Street a quiet abode with two bedrooms. Their church made arrangements for the first three months to be rent free. The street was near the waterfront that has undergone a dramatic resurgence.

Tall office buildings and condominiums with views of New York's skyscrapers have been erected. It's a dramatic change from an industrial section, where my father once worked. The impact of the restoration of the area has also expanded to several streets in the area.

There's a new mall nearby and popular restaurants have sprung up, blending the old and the new, as well as expanded shopping where once there were only industrial buildings and bars. The area has taken on an entirely new appearance that has put Jersey City at the forefront of redevelopment.

I went to view the change of the waterfront and the Gap, a popular area where I went swimming with my brother Paul. I walked along the waterfront to see its renewal at a narrow point of the Hudson River, where New York buildings seem possible to reach out and touch. We thought it was always that way, but not as dramatic as it is today.

"Wow," was all I could say.

13

The Roarin' 20's

If America ever had a frivolous era, it was the 1920's, when jobs were plentiful and easy spending was the norm, at least for the nation's elite income earners.

My mother said my father was content working at an oil refinery. He described it as a happy time. He arose every day anxious to go to go to work, except he was not earning enough to be free of the pressure for rent, food and services.

With three growing boys, my mother insisted their primary need for rooms was a place with three bedrooms. A house was the solution, but my father was afraid of paying for a mortgage. As long as he could afford the cost my father was content and my mother too.

In the midst of an economic boom, Prohibition was enacted to ban the sale and consumption of liquor and beer, but it did not stop people from drinking. Bootleggers were bringing liquor into the country to sell at illegal bars and clubs called "speakeasies."

They were not on every street corner, but not hard to find despite the attempts to hide them. The ones in New York usually had upscale furnishings that added to their appeal and offset the cost of liquor. The speakeasies had strict rules to maintain their secrecy, but it amused customers. They felt it was often overdone, except the caution to protect them from legal authorities was never ignored.

Prohibition was a boon to bootleggers, but social drinkers hated it. To ban a drink or two at dinner was an imposition to the polite way they lived. According to the *Hudson Reporter*, some cafes in the city had an approach to the problem Prohibition had imposed. At lunch, alcoholic beverages were not served, but an alcoholic drink was included with dinner, if it was ordered.

It seemed to be a reasonable solution.

Social drinkers did not go to speakeasies in Jersey City. Many of them were in vacant tenements or basement rooms that didn't suit them. The whiskey was cheap, but the décor was below the standard social drinkers liked. It would have suited immigrant labourers in the city. They were willing to sacrifice ambiance for cheap whiskey, and did not need plush surroundings to do it. My father with several Rusyn friends including Irish immigrants they knew avoided a speakeasy. Instead, they pooled their resources and bought a bottle of "booze," a word immigrants liked, for a Friday night get together. Once, a couple of young thugs accosted my father with the intent to rob him on his way home after one of their parties.

He had to run or fight.

Friday was payday and he was carrying a lot of cash, so he decided to fight. He pulled his cap down tight and spit in the palms of his hands, as he did when he had work to do, but this time he cupped them into fists to be ready to fight.

After the skirmish with the tugs, he arrived home with a black eye and a cut on his cheek, but his pay envelope was in his cap, where he put it in the event of such an encounter. He celebrated his resiliency with my mother over a drink at home.

"See, Anyce," he said, "I'm a tough American."

"A smart one, too," she replied.

The impact of Prohibition on the social structure of the nation was significant, but it was also a negative edict. The country survived, but it took a decade to do it. Soon innovations were introduced in the movies, travel and sports that gave the economy a needed spurt.

Thanks to Henry Ford's success with his assembly line production, it was being duplicated in other industries that brought jobs to urban areas. My father was impressed with the automobile, but he preferred to call it a car. Several events were still being discussed in the ensuing decade. Everyone remained thrilled by Lindbergh's nonstop solo flight to Paris that helped advance the development of commercial aviation. In sports, Babe Ruth established a home run record that started a march of success for the New York Yankees that increased the interest in Major League baseball. In college sports, the Four Horsemen of Notre Dame and Red Grange of Illinois excited football fans long after their gridiron accomplishments.

In home entertainment, the new rage was a plastic disc called a record that played music and vocals everyone wanted to hear from a hand cranked player. Now, the jazz of Louis Armstrong could be heard at home and many couples were dancing the Charleston, but nothing characterized the era more than young women, called "flappers," doing their versions of the dance. Lastly, at the end of the 1920's, the first talking movie was shown. It was only a short rendition by the singer Al Jolson, but it was enough for movie goers to demand "the talkies."

Aside from knowing about Charles Lindbergh and Babe Ruth, my parents did not follow the news, except for what my mother heard at the grocery or my father at work. He knew about jazz recordings, but he liked to listen to accordion records that were played to a Polka. My brothers said he thought the Charleston was tame, but loved to demonstrate the dance with my mother in our front room.

Another insight into the decade was the different meaning given to words to explain people, places and things that had not been used before. The words soon became a part of a new vernacular in the way that the nation's youth have expanded the use of abbreviated words in internet messaging. They are important to understand the independent mood of the 1920's with an impact that continued into the 1930's.

Some of the examples include the following: If someone said you were "all wet," it had nothing to do with water. It simply meant you were wrong.

A "blind date" described someone you had never met before. It was a rare occurrence in the previous decade.

A "scapegoat" was a person who was blamed for something he or she had not done, except it usually referred to a male.

To have a "crush" on a guy or girl meant you were in love with someone, who did not know it or did not care.

A "bull session" was a casual group discussion, not a gathering of male bovines.

The term "bumped off" did not refer to being pushed from a trolley or bus seat. It had a more serious implication that someone was murdered probably by a gangster.

The most unusual designations were for a lady's legs and feet called gams or hoofs, but no one knew why. Some women said they barked, but it was an explanation after women stood in tight shoes for long periods or walked too far carrying groceries.

It was a logical explanation.

My parents paid little attention to the different meaning of new words, except for swell, which meant something was pleasant or agreeable. It was introduced in the 1920's and became America's favorite idiom. A girl or a guy could be described as "swell," as well as a movie or date, but like some words it has lost its popularity.

John said everyone had a positive attitude about the decade because of a growing economy, until the explosive day in November, 1929 when the Stock Market crashed. There was also a concern over the low wages paid workers. It brought about the expansion of labor unions that became a political issue.

Some things never change.

Coal continued to be a revered fuel in the 1920's as a way to heat homes and business offices. It was brought by train to a storage yard jn the city around the corner from Bright Street. The train had to climb up an incline that forced it to make a slow stop and go into the yard. The move up the incline caused the rail cars to ram each other, spilling coal onto the tracks that produced the source of free fuel for a large number of eager scavengers.

According to John there was no schedule for the coal train's arrival, only an unofficial watch that alerted everyone when it had arrived, and the rush was on to pick up the coal. The need for the free fuel was popular with low wage earners during the era's affluent period of frivolity. It may have been an early indication of what was ahead for the economy in the next decade, but no one noticed it.

When John was only fifteen, he saw an opportunity to make money delivering coal. With Mike's help, he collected enough of the "black gold" at the train tracks for our use at home and for his business. He soon had a bevy of customers to deliver the coal to that helped keep their business locations warm. He used pull carts he made from wood boxes and discarded tricycle tires. His first customer was Jim Keegan, who owned the stable, but complained that his office was cold in winter and had a coal burning stove installed.

He knew that anthracite coal left more long lasting embers that kept his office warmer than burning wood. John sold only anthracite coal and erected a storage area in the back of the stable, which was convenient. On cold days, he could burn four full pails of coal, and sometimes more. John made sure he delivered the extra coal when he needed it.

It was a profitable arrangement for a teenager. Jim Keegan called John the best coal suppler he ever had, adding that all he needed was an ice delivery business and he would be working for him.

Problems arose when grocery stores began selling coal in sealed bags. That innovation and a competitive price was enough to take away John's delivery advantage. It wasn't long before his business came to an end, but Jim Keegan did not want to carry coal bags and remained his sole customer.

Mike continued doing odd jobs at the stable, pitching hay, feeding the horses and mucking out stalls. When people came with Kodak box cameras to take pictures, he would pose holding a pitchfork. The amateur photographers liked including him in their photos, and as a gesture of goodwill he would take them on a tour of the stable. They would usually give him a dime tip for his extra service. When he told Jim Keegan about the tour, he had a positive response.

"Great," he said. "It'll make me famous."

John left high school to get a job where he could learn a trade. Getting a job was not a problem in the 1920's before the Market's plunge, but the pay was never sufficient. John worked at a small printing shop, but within a year it went out of business. The rent was too high and the shop too small to be able to compete. He worked at other jobs, including stints at a commercial bakery, a machine shop and a pencil factory.

Like John, Mike left school to get a job. He had several minor stints, but his favourite was with a steamship company. He worked to help refurbish cruise ships after they returned from a tour at sea. He longed to become a world traveller, but the job didn't last and his dream to travel was short lived.

When the Stock Market crashed, the economy went into a tail spin. The boom times in America were over and it would take almost the next decade for the country to recover. People were concerned, despite assurances from Washington. They worried they would not be able to keep up with ordinary living, especially low paid immigrant labourers. My mother worked at part time jobs to help with family expenses, but it was never enough.

There were few jobs until Franklin D. Roosevelt was elected president. After several years, he ordered the production of arms to aid Britain in its conflict with the Germans, which pleased the British, but some Americans opposed the move. The military build-up helped the economy. People said it increased our readiness for any conflict. It proved to be an important development for the preparation to World War II.

If the Roarin'20's were years of near fantasy, the decade that followed was a time of harsh reality. When the economy collapsed, all that was left was the music of jazz that continued to be played on record players, as the people yearned for a return of the prosperity they once knew called "the good old days."

14

The Thirties

Despite the Stock Market crash, the swift movement of paperwork on transactions was still essential. Mike was told the Stock Exchange was hiring "runners." They were called to deliver records to and from banks and brokerage firms. He felt delivering reports with stock data required no special talent and made his way to Wall Street, except being a "runner" was an entry level job often reserved for college graduates and not easy to get.

Mike was street savvy with a pleasant temperament that made him positive about getting a job. My mother said it came about when he turned eighteen. He rode the nickel ferry to Battery Park and walked to Wall Street. The day was overcast and fit the mood he encountered from several runners. They were far from friendly and called him an intruder, trying to take away one of their jobs. Their reaction surprised him and a confrontation filled him with concern. Later when he came home he gave a report on what happened that depressed my father.

"It was a bad day," Mike simple said.

Many of his friends continued to feel New York was a Mecca for jobs, but that viewpoint did not hold up long. John and Paul remained positive, doing their best to boost Mike's morale, but after his visit to Wall Street he realized the country's problems were difficult everywhere, including New York. Later, when John told me about Mike's visit to the Stock Exchange, it was hard not to feel his disappointed, but I felt proud of him. It seemed he was always willing to take on tough assignments, but his experience in New York did not ease Mike's concerns

An increase in new tariff laws made the economy worse. It seemed workers and business executives were both victims of layoffs in every industry. Finding a job was nearly impossible. It didn't take long before everyone's concerns became a reality. With the growing demand for gasoline, the oil refinery where my father worked had minimal layoffs, but he worried about a pay cut.

It increased his concern.

Following the confrontation with the runners, Mike left Wall Street to go to Union Square, where labor groups gathered to protest the breakdown in the economy. The trek was longer than the one he made from the ferry to the financial district, but he was in good physical condition and young enough to walk the distance. He said it refreshed him. At Union Square, public speakers were actively berating financiers and bankers, who they held responsible for the country's economic collapse.

According to Mike's report, it did not take long for the crowd to become aroused. He was sure a physical outburst was about to happen. It did and the police were called to restore order, but he was upset when some demonstrators who did not participate in a fracas were treated harshly. It was not the kind of day he had expected, but Mike was told that it was a common scene at Union Square.

He was upset with the runners he met on Wall Street, but he was more annoyed over the reaction of the police at Union Square. According to John, the events seemed to rob him of his enthusiasm and he was sorry he had gone to New York. He was a young man, but he had a studied insight into business and politics, even at his early age. Like my father, he was concerned the economy was not going to improve soon. Similar to other young men caught in the devastating economic collapse he did not know what to do. He only hoped it would improve,

To everyone's dismay the economy got worse.

Every business suffered, except insurance firms and Hollywood studios, as both recorded large profits. Movie ticket receipts increased after the introduction of sound to motion pictures. Film moguls anticipated a boost in business that "talking pictures" would bring, but they did not expect the bonanza that occurred. The profits soared from the public's response to films when they could hear the actor's voice on the screen. By the early

1930's, studio heads and movie stars were among the top money earners.

Escape from reality has always been an antidote to ease economic distress, and a Depression plagued public was eager for a respite from their problems. What better place to find it than at a movie theater, where it was said that for as little as a nickel or a dime you could forget your troubles.

As for insurance firms, their performance was not as profitable, but people had more confidence to protect their money with insurance investments than what they got from banks.

A positive move for my family occurred when John got a job at Federal Shipbuilding in Kearny, New Jersey that made him a celebrity in the neighborhood. Everyone wanted to know how he did it, but there was no secret. He was persistent and kept going back to the shipyard until one day a need arose and he was hired. Soon other young men from Bright Street went there to apply for a job. Several were hired, but what was more important, John gave most of his earnings to my mother to help my parents alleviate financial problems.

Mike said John was a born leader, and several promotions at the shipyard proved it.When he was less than thirty years old, he was named an assistant superintendent of the Ship Fitting Department. The primary group that built destroyers for the U.S. Navy Later, with the war looming, the building of destroyers became a critical need.

Once, John got a special invitation for us to witness a launching. Pete, my father and I went to see a new destroyer slide into the water for the first time. John's boss said that because of his efforts the ship had been completed ahead of schedule. He called it the kind of effort the President wanted.

I thought John had been contacted by President Roosevelt, but he said his boss had only repeated a reference from a speech he made. I stuck with my first impression and told my friends John had gotten a message from the President. They were impressed and wanted to hear all about how destroyers were built. I said I did not know how they were made, but it was exciting to see a launching, as the ship slid into the water after a bottle of champagne was smashed across its bow.

15

Fistfights

There were times in elementary school when I was involved in trivial disputes that had to be settled by a fistfight. I was being threatened, shoved or called a bad name. It reached a point where a fistfight could not be avoided. I didn't want to be labled a coward and had to answer the challenge. It was like a shootout in a western film, but without the guns, except before the fight could start a stick had to be knocked off the challenger's shoulder.

I thought it was a tedious ritual.

Sometimes unexpected things happened to cause a fight. Once, a neighbor named Billy punched me in the stomach when I wasn't expecting it. We were in the third grade walking with our fathers and not a word passed between us, but as they finished conversing and saying goodbye, Billy hit me in the stomach. I wanted to tell my father what happened, but he was walking away with his father smirking. I was upset and had to struggle to catch my breath, but I was determined to avenge his sneak punch.

I told Mike what happened and he encouraged me to get even with Billy. The next day I went to confront him. He was with several friends squatting at the curb drawing in the street with chalk. I thought of what Mike said I should do and gave him a hard shove that sent him sprawling. He recovered and looked up at me with a startled, annoyed expression.

"Oh, it's you," he said surprised.

"Yeah," I said, trying to sound tough.

When he got up, I socked him, and I didn't need a stick to knock off his shoulder to do it. I told his friends he started the confrontation with a sneak punch, so it was within the rules of the street to retaliate. We did everything by the rules and getting even for a sneak punch was one of them.

After I hit him, he started to cry and his father came out shouting I had attacked his son. I tried to tell him Billy hit me first, but he would not listen to me. Several days later, we played together at school. He didn't mention our scuffle, but he never hit me in the stomach again, either.

I had another street fight with a neighbor named Johnny Pazheski. It started over a minor incident, but it turned into a quarrel that had to be settled with physical combat. Johnny and I had always been friends and we played together, sometimes with his younger brother Charlie. A disagreement led him to challenge me to a fistfight, except he first had to find a stick to knock off my shoulder.

Here we go again, I thought.

I waited patiently, while he searched for a piece of wood, except it took a long time. I thought we were going to have to call off the fight, but he finally came back with a stick. After he knocked it off my shoulder he swung at me, but I moved quickly and he missed me. I swung back and hit him with a solid blow that knocked him down. It might have been a different fight if he had not missed me, but my solid punch took away his confidence.

Every time Johnny came at me he seemed to swing and miss, but I was able to hit him with a hard punch. A few times, I hit him several times and his nose started to bleed. His father came out. I thought the fight was over, but he was angry and encouraged Johnny to continue fighting.

That was okay with me, but his brother Charlie came at me. He swung a quick punch the same way Johnny did, but I stepped aside for it to glance off my shoulder. I retaliated with a punch to his jaw that stunned him and Mike came out again. He told them the fight was over and to go home, which they did. The next day Johnny and I were friends again, which pleased me. I wanted to tell him about my objection to getting a stick to knock off my shoulder, but I let it pass.

I never told him about my going to the Woodier House, a recreation club established to develop friendly relationships and fair play among the youth of the area. I spent most of my time wrestling, but I did attend several boxing sessions. I don't know how it fit into their program, except the lessons helped me in my fistfights, but it was not as much fun as wrestling.

It's important not to give the wrong impression about my fistfights. There were many I did not win and most involved a neighbor we called Buster. He was a bully who always tried to take advantage of someone physically smaller, which was why no one liked him. He was three years older than me and bigger than I was, so it was easy for him to take advantage of me. He could handle himself in a fight, but he was not as tough as other kids in the neighborhood, except he always tried to portray a tough image.

He had straight blond hair, as well as thin lanky legs and arms that kept me from getting close to hitting him. He had a bad temper and when Buster got mad, he got mean. I once head butted him in the stomach hard enough to knock him down. I jumped on him and put my hands around his neck to choke him, but he was too strong for me and broke loose. After choking him, I knew he would be waiting for me to get even, so I delayed going home. My father sent Pete to get me. I told him about knocking Buster down and choking him.

"Good," he said. "Don't be afraid of him."

That was easy for him to say. He was bigger than Buster, who was no match for Pete. We walked home at a fast pace, but he was waiting for me like a hunter stalking his prey, except when he saw Pete he quickly went inside his rooms. I laughed because if there was one person Buster feared, it was Pete. The next day he acted as if nothing happened, just as Johnny and Billy did after our fights. It seemed all my skirmishes never carried over to the next day.

One afternoon, Buster and I were scavenging in the lot behind our rooms, not knowing what we wanted to do when several kids approached us. The leader went directly to Buster and accused him of stealing coal from his brother on the tracks to the storage yard. His voice had a threatening tone that could be a precursor to a bad situation. He seemed tougher than any of the local gang members I knew. They were bad characters, but not as mean as this guy. I was sure the situation meant trouble.

"Ain't you the kid that took coal from my "brudder," he asked Buster?

"Not me," Buster said.

Some infractions were tolerated on the street, but stealing coal from a neighbor was not one of them. I was certain there was going to be trouble, but I hoped I did not end up being included in something Buster should not have done.

What a jerk, I said to myself.

"I never stole any coal," Buster repeated.

"He said you had blonde hair."

"Yeah, so what," Buster retorted.

"It means you're the guy."

"Whadda do, dye it," a gang member asked?

"No, I don't dye it," Buster sneered.

"He's a sissy," another gang member said.

"What are you jealous," Buster challenged.

He should not have said that. Only girls dyed their hair and the reply riled one of the gang. I was sure things were going to get worse.

"Hit him," someone said,

Suddenly, the leader hit Buster with a hard punch that sent him sprawling into the weeds.

"C'mon, get up," he yelled. "I'm gonna teach ya not to steal coal from my brudder."

Buster was crying. I had never seen him cry before, but it was no use. The tough kid hit him again, but now his friends were nervous. They looked around to see if anyone was passing the lot. I could not stand by any longer and watch this gang leader beat up Buster.

"Don't hit him anymore," I said.

Mike told me to always keep quiet when I was in trouble. I should have listened to him, but I played the hero and hoped it was not a mistake. The tough kid hesitated, but stared at me, as if I was going to be his next victim.

"Is he your brudder," he asked me?

"Are you kidding? I don't have blond hair."

He laughed and I knew from his reaction I was not going to be included in Buster's problem. I was glad I had come to his defense. What the heck, he was a neighbor, despite the number of times he hit me over some petty incident, but what happened next turned the episode into an embarrassing experience.

He told his friends to hold Buster down.

What now, I wondered?

Despite Buster's resistance, he took off his pants and began to take his shorts. His friends encouraged him to do it, but I thought he had gone too far and had enough of this tough guy's routine. To remove his shorts angered me. I spoke up again, but I worried over his coming after me.

"Don't take his underwear," I said in a strong, commanding voice, feeling sure of myself.

He paused with a puzzled look, but he didn't complete his final insult. He left leaving Buster with his underwear, except he kept the pants. I was glad to see him go, but he did not run away. He just walked slowly with a defiant strut, but Buster never hesitated. He sprung up and sprinted to the fence at his backyard and climbed over it faster than I had ever seen him do it before. Later, he acted as if nothing happened, but I was sure he was glad no one witnessed the skirmish.

I told Pete about the incident.

"If he stole the coal, he got off easy," he said.

"He stole the coal," I said.

"How do you know? Did you see him do it?"

"No, but I know Buster," I said.

There was someone else I knew we called Slick, who was also a troublemaker. I didn't have a fistfight with him, but I came close. He promoted his nickname and even used it when he did his school work, except his teaches insisted that he write his full name on his assignments.

He followed the order, but continued to include his nickname. He lived around the corner from where we had moved and always seemed to be doing weird things. He had a mean attitude that kept him from having any friends. The tough guys on Bright Street would never have put up with his antics

I made up my mind to avoid him.

One day, I went to play baseball with some friends to an area we called the "Triangle" It was as interesting a field to play on as it is to describe. It was located alongside train tracks that ran from Journal Square past the Triangle onto an elevated train track and then down into a tunnel under the Hudson River to New York. The Triangle was a safe distance from the rail tracks. We made sure of that. We only wanted to play on its soft surface.

Mostly, we played on small, uneven rock strewn lots or city streets, where automobile traffic was a problem, but neither traffic nor scattered rocks were a concern at the Triangle. There was nothing else like it nearby. It obviously got its name from its shape, but its isolation added to its attraction. To get to it, we had to go down a steep hill at the end of a dead end street. On the field, we made home plate at its narrow end that was more than 200 feet to center field and almost the same distance to left and right field.

One day, we went to the Triangle to play ball, except we didn't have enough players for a game. We were only going to hit and toss the ball, but someone made the mistake of asking Slick to join us. We took turns rotating positions. When my turn came to hit, Slick was pitching. It did not take long for him to start an unnecessary fracas.

He threw several pitches too far from home plate. I stood ready to hit. Someone yelled for him to get the ball over. He did everything he could to be disruptive and threw the next pitch straight at my legs. The ball hit me in the thigh. It hurt and made me angry, but he didn't care. I knew he aimed it at me. He threw another pitch that forced me to jump back to avoid being hit again.

I knew he aimed at me

I was irate, especially when he started laughing over his antics, so I called him some bad names. Someone yelled for him to stop being a jerk and get the ball over the plate. It didn't help. His next pitch just cleared my shoulder. I had to duck away quickly to avoid being hit in the head. He had no regard for fair play and did not care if he hit me with the baseball.

That was it for me.

I had enough of his irresponsible behavior. I ran after him with the bat, but I could not get close enough to hit him with it, so I threw it at him. He jumped, but the bat hit him in the legs and he fell down hard. Now, I was laughing, but throwing the bat was a big mistake. He got up and threw it back at me. It didn't reach me and our confrontation turned into a standoff. I only wished I had the chance to hit him with the baseball. He left arguing with several of my friends, hurling vile curses at all of us.

I was glad to see him go. I thought he would he was a trouble maker, who was in the need of mental help. Who invited him to play ball with us, I asked? No one answered, but I vowed never to play with him again.

Once was enough for me.

Later, my friend Lee Bracey, who lived several doors from me had a similar confrontation with him that ended in a fistfight. I was glad to hear that Lee beat him in the fight and won the confrontation.

Maybe Slick was not a lucky nickname, but no one cared.

16
Our Rooms

Most people in the city called where they lived rooms, not apartments. Since Bright Street was not far from the waterfront, we said we were near the "docks" and everyone knew where we meant.

I lived on Bright Street until I was ten years old, but in different rooms. One was at a two story wood house at 67 Bright Street, but we later moved to a tenement on the street at number 71. They were almost next door to each other, but a world apart in many other ways.

We lived at 67 Bright Street until I was seven, but the rooms had several major problems. We had no central heat. Our warmth came from the kitchen stove. We had no electricity with wall plugs and used lighted Kerosene lamps that were a danger of a fire. Lastly, we had no hot running water.

After coming home from work, my father liked to converse in the kitchen with my mother and brothers. The warm stove was an important part of the. sessions Our stove was a muscular relic that were similar to ones at a country farm house. It had black slotted covers that were lifted out to feed the hungry beast with fire wood. We often relied on discarded wood for the stove we got from a nearby lumber mill. Pete made friends with the mill workers getting sandwiches for their lunch from a deli without accepting a tip. They would give him extra wood scraps for his help that we took home. It pleased my mother when she saw our cart filled with wood. My father was over joyed with Pete's exploits.

Usually, when I came home to 67 Bright Street in the winter hungry and cold from playing in the snow, my mother placed a small bench next to the opened oven door to rest my frozen feet, as I sipped a hot bowl of Campbell's tomato soup. The warm oven provided a pleasant relief from the frigid day and the soup tasted like a magical broth.

A heavy snowfall once soaked through the flat roof on our rooms at 67 Bright Street that leaked on the stove. After a strong complaint, the roof was recoated and the leaks stopped. Besides the lack of heat, we had no hot water or electricity. You can imagine what that was like. Over the next several years, it seemed the roof needed repaire, but it didn't take long to do such a simply problem.

Early construction in city followed a simple pattern. Wood framed houses came first, expanding inland from the river, but it did not take long for sturdy brownstones to be built. They were costly, but a sought after residence. To fill the need of a growing immigrant population, less costly red brick buildings called tenements were built. We moved into one of on the second floor at 71 Bright Street that had heat, hot water and electric power.

To tell you about Bright Street, I have to start with a candy store at the near corner. It had a dust ridden window display of smiling cigarette smokers that would be out of place today. The store was owned by Mr. Rosen, who wore a light gray cotton jacket that made him look like a department store clerk, but he was a patient man that everyone liked. The store sold newspapers, cigarettes, candy and a host of five and ten cent items, plus a kite I wanted that cost $.25 cents my father said was too much to spend for a toy.

A rotating fan was the store's main feature. On hot summer days my friends and I went in to the store to be relieved by the cool breeze of a fan. A neighborhood gang had the same idea, but they often harassed Mr. Rosen. He called the police to expel them. I once had a run in with several gang members outside the store. I ended up with a black eye, but it was worth it. The scuffle made me a hero on the street and a favourite of Mr. Rosen. A grocery was at the opposite corner, where my mother did her food shopping. It was convenient, but I liked going to it because she always bought me a box of cookies. They had a graham cracker base with a soft marshmallow covered with chocolate. It was a special treat beyond compare and I craved them.

Sam Grossman was the proprietor, a quiet man with a polite manner, who came from Eastern Europe and spoke my mother's language. It made the grocery her favorite store, as well as her shopping easier when they conversed in their native language. I liked him almost as much as Mr. Rosen.

He was a short man with a round face and a fringe of gray hair. He had eye glasses with a thin metal frame and wore a newly washed white shirt with a starched collar every day, including a thin black tie and a full length cleaned apron. I mentioned his daily ensemble to my mother and when we got to the store he had on his usual attire.

"See," I said, and she smiled.

It's hard to imagine, but it was a time when street peddlers sold fruit, vegetables, furniture and clothing from horse drawn wagons. There was an excitement when they arrived and housewives hurried to the street to make a purchase. They were like a horde of shoppers at a store sale, but what I liked were the calls the vendors made to announce their arrival.

Several renditions were only a single word theme, but some were long phrases that left no doubt about what they were selling. At first, I paid no attention to the peddlers, but a view from our tenement always got my attention and I listened to the announcements of their arrivals. It was a special street show.

The sales call I liked was made by the clothing peddler. It was an ordinary message compared to what the fruit and vegetable peddlers shouted, but it had an unusual flair and intonation. "Suits for sale and dresses, too" he announced in a loud voice. He elongated the double vowel in the word suits, as if it was an operatic aria. I thought it was a special vocal presentation he did to be creative, but to make a sale meant more than just his call.

I longed to imitate him.

One day it was my turn from one of our windows. "Soots," I shouted, as loud as the peddler, but I skipped any reference to the word dresses, except I repeated the call "Soots." No one cared and I gave up my imitation.

To service the street peddler's horses, there was Keegan's stable across the street from the grocery, less than a block from our rooms. The stable was an important part of the neighborhood, both positive and negative, but it was fun to play in the loft. Pete said he enjoyed it, too. I was sorry we had to leave when the horses were brought back to the stable.

Overall, the most important announcement came from the ice man. There were families uptown with new refrigerators, but not on Bright Street. We had an ice box and relied on the ice man to keep our food fresh. It made him a special visitor. His deliveries were based on the size of the ice box. He came with little fanfare, except for the usual loud pronouncement when he arrived.

"The ice man could clearly be heard throughout the street, but delivering the ice was not an easy task. I marvelled at the strength he displayed to carry such a heavy load. He used large tongs for even a medium piece of ice. If it was a large cut of ice, he lifted it to his shoulder, where he had placed a rubber pad to absorb the cold, wet load he carried.

An average block of ice lasted a week or more and cost twenty five cents, plus ten cents to carry it to the ice box. Some families had only a wooden vat under the sink, where they kept their food. They only needed a small piece of ice that they carried home. In winter, people without an ice box put food on a fire escape to keep from spoiling, but in the summer you could not live without the ice man. There was only a small difference of the need for ice in the summer and in the winter.

No one had storm windows on Bright Street. One winter the front room window panes at 67 Bright Street were frozen with white swirling icy patterns. They looked like designs by an artist, but they could also have a troubling result. The window panes cracked and cold winds were quick to invade the front room. They had to be boarded up, which made the room dark, but warmer until new glass panes were installed. John wanted to leave the boards on until spring. He hated the cold and called the front room "Siberia." It was a cleaver line, but my mother didn't like it.

Winters were difficult, but not only from the lack of central heat. We had no running hot water and heated water on the stove to take to the tub for our baths. Heating the water was not a problem, but to lug it to the bathroom was a chore.

As a young boy, I took a bath in a large cbasin my mother set up in the kitchen. It was easier than carting water, but I preferred the bathtub with hot water. What was worse, we had no electricity and used kerosene lamps, which was another problem. A large part of the country was putting up with the same problems, but we solved most of ours when we moved to 71 Bright Street.

We still called our parlor the front room. To us it was a room with fancy drapes, but we only had shades and curtains on the windows, without drapes. A used RCA Victrola was added to the room that played one 78 rpm record at a time, but we didn't have a radio, which I missed. We had a sofa, but no soft chair. We brought two chairs from the dining room to place at the front room windows. They fit the space and became permanent fixtures.

After dinner, my father would listen to Polka music on a record player, and smoked his pipe with Ivanhoe tobacco. He was a light smoker and never inhaled. The pack only cost a nickel that would last a week. He added an apple slice to the tobacco to keep it fresh and give the mixture a special flavor.

Our rooms provided shelter where needs were satisfied by necessity, especially at 67 Bright Street. The kerosene lamps provided an eerie glow, especially when it got dark. I hated its pungent odor, but a possible fire worried my mother.

We were excited when we moved to 71 Bright Street. It was a tenement, but it had the improvements we needed, including electric lights with wall switches and steam heat from radiators that hissed and banged, but made our rooms warm. We also had hot running water that made everyone happy.

The rooms had three bed rooms, a kitchen, dining room and a parlour. My mother was happy, which pleased my father. Of course, it took John to support the move. My brothers did a lot of repainting and put a synthetic covering on the kitchen walls with a small flowery pattern. With a cheerful kitchen that was bright and inviting our spirits were the same.

I liked living in a brick building, and to help pay the rent, my father tended the basement furnace that heated each unit. We were not plagued in the winter when it was cold, bit no longer a problem. It was a significant move, but I was glad we stayed on Bright Street.

17

Diversions

In the 1930's, America wanted to dance and a clarinet playing band leader named, Benny Goodman, helped them do it with a new interpretation of jazz called "Swing."

\When Glenn Miller, another popular band leader added his musical style for young couples to dance, the big band era began. Soon, more people were dancing in ball rooms, social clubs and school gyms than in any other decade. Dancing became one of the most popular diversions to offset the ills of the Depression.

The early dances were carryovers from the 1920's, including the Fox Trot, Shag and Peabody. They had an upbeat tempo and popular throughout the 1930's and 1940's. It took a lot of practice to master their intricate steps, especially the Shag and Peabody. Like most men at the time, John loved to dance, but it was more than a hobby to him. He was practical about most things, but a perfectionist when it came to dancing. It started when he was sixteen and won a dance contest doing the Shag.

He was hooked. I would watch him practice dancing like an Olympic athlete, except it was for his Saturday night soirees. His routine included holding the back of a chair, while he did the short, but rapid hop steps of the Shag until it became a part of him. He then switched to the long gliding moves of the Peabody. He introduced Pete to the joy of dancing and he won a contest doing the Peabody.

Their dancing could not compare to what happened on one of our Sunday drives. We were in Belmar, a popular Jersey Shore resort, strolling on the boardwalk, including John, my mother and father, Pete and I. We were enjoying the cool ocean breeze, but my mother said she was tired and needed to rest before we left for home. We went to an open air dance pavilion to have sodas at the bar.

It seemed too early for dancing, but there were several interested customers across from us, including an attractive young blonde. She was tall and slender and hard not to notice. It was early evening and a jukebox was playing an instrumental tune. Hearing the music was all the encouragement John needed to ask her to dance. She hesitated, saying she did not want to be the only one dancing, but after some polite coaxing she relented with a smile.

Watching him practice dancing using the back of a chair, I was anxious to see him do it with a live partner, especially someone as pretty as this girl. Pete said he would have liked to dance with her. It was easy to see why. She was attractive and I would have liked to dance with, herself myself, if I was a lot older.

A jukebox was playing a musical rendition with a Peabody beat. John led her effortlessly through its strident steps and intricate turns. It was exciting, as passing strollers stopped to watch them. When they finished, everyone in the pavilion applauded, as well as the strollers. There were shouts of "more" from the crowd for another dance.

John and his attractive partner obliged and he led her effortlessly, as if he was Fred Astaire. When the dance was over she hugged him and they parted. As he headed toward us, she stared at him with an appreciative glance. I did, too. I now knew he was a good dancer that made me feel his practice sessions with a chair were worthwhile.

"Let's go" was all he said after a sip of soda.

It wasn't long before the Shag and Peabody were passé and the Lindy Hop became the most popular dance. The "Lindy" has quick moves that are done to a fast beat, but they did not include a hop step, unless they were added by the dancers. Teenagers started doing the Lindy in the 1920's as an adaptation of the Charleston, but it was not until the1930's that they were "jitter bugging" their way across America and didn't stop until decades later.

Some dances represented the wild side of music, but nothing could erase the need for soft ballads. They never lost their appeal. America's youth wanted to dance to music with a slow beat that would express the romantic lyrics with the arms of a male dancer around his favourite girl. The songs had a personal meaning with titles such as, "That Old Feeling, I'll Never Smile Again and Love Walked In."

Early in the 1940's, Tommy Dorsey, added a vocalist to his band from Hoboken. He sang the romantic ballads that thrilled audiences, especially young women and female teenagers. Of course, the singer was Frank Sinatra. John met him early in his career through a friend named, Dick Pattela. John helped him get a job at the shipyard that he sorely needed to get out of debt.

Dick was a tall, good looking and an excellent dancer. He was the type of guy who always had an entourage of women following him on and off the dance floor. What he lacked was a car, but John had one that was essential to party on weekends. It wasn't long before John was ferrying a group from Jersey City to obscure night clubs to applaud Frank Sinatra, who was destined to become America's favourite vocalist.

One of the key members of the group was Tony Barbato, the brother of Frank Sinatra's future wife, Nancy. It was easy for John to mix with Sinatra. Later, after an appearance at the Rustic Cabin, a North Jersey Night Club propelled him to stardom, so John and his car were no longer needed.

I asked him what he thought of Sinatra. He said he liked him, but thought his voice was too weak to make it as a popular vocalist. I was a big Frank Sinatra fan and felt John may have been a good dancer, but he was no judge of singing talent.

As much as America wanted to dance, there was no holding them back from singing. They were abetted by Radio "disc jockeys" playing the vocals the nation wanted to hear. In New York, the leading DJ was William B. Williams with his daily program called the "Make Believe Ballroom."

He dominated the airways with Frank Sinatra vocals, and referred to him as the "Chairman of the Board," among all the popular singers. It became the most listened to radio music show in New York. There were also brochures available for a dime called "Song Sheets" with the lyrics America wanted to sing. It was a small price to pay to help amateurcr crooners, male and female, learn the words of songs to sing at parties and to each other.

The most important diversion for high school teenagers was the Senior Prom. It has a history that began in the 1800's when debutantes were presented at social affairs and promenaded around a dance floor with their escorts. High school seniors would later imitate society in formal attire at a special dance they called the Prom.

Male Prom goers usually had to work at odd jobs to get the money to rent a tuxedo for the event, which was essential, as well as a corsage for female dates in a new gown. The costs were far more than what the girl's parents paid than what it cost male parents. At times, the Prom has evolved into a social event.

When Pete went to his Prom, it was a must to go to a New York nightclub that made my father smile. It added to the expense, but no one wanted to miss an evening at a night club to dance to a renowned band leader's music. The high school dance ended at 11:00 PM, but Prom goers often left at 10:00 PM to make it to a night club for at least an hour or more. The Prom concluded with an early breakfast in Bickford's at Journal Square. It was a tradition most Prom goers followed, if the girl was allowed to stay out that late.

A car was necessary for the Prom, but it could be a problem. There were no rental cars. The family car could be was the first test, but getting it was not easy. Sometimes a "double date" with someone who had the use of the family car was available. My brother John drove a Buick Road Master, an impressive car that was white with a black roof.

Did I forget to say perfect?

John's Buick was all Pete needed to take his high school sweetheart, Virginia, who later became his wife went to the Glenn Island Casino on Long Island, a top rated club to dance to the music of Glenn Miller, playing his favourite renditions for guests to dance the Peabody. Pete loved it and nodded his pleasure to Glenn Miller, who responded with a quick salute.

18

The Movies

While dancing and song sheets provided diversions for adults during the Depression, I usually got my kicks at the movies and went to the Palace near Bright Street. It cost a nickel for kids on Saturday matinees, while the Capitol an upgrade charged a dime. It was a small difference, but important to my mother, as well as being a long walk to the Capitol.

There was one thing we didn't like about the Palace. On Saturday, anxious young matinee movie goers from five to ten years old created an overflow. We were ushered to the balcony to sit two to a seat. Pete was older and bigger than me, so he got his own seat. What made the Palace popular were the two films we saw, including a main feature and a western, plus a newsreel, a cartoon and a "serial" of ten segments. With everything on the screen plus the five cents I saved going to the Palace, I bought a bag of popcorn. It made the Palace my favourite movie theater, despite sitting two to a seat.

The largest and most popular theaters in the city were at the Square, where top rated films were shown before they made it downtown. During the week, a film at the Square cost thirty five cents for adults and fifteen cents for children, but more on weekends.

The Jersey Journal, the city's daily newspaper, relocated to the area before it was named "Journal Square" after the paper, but it was easier to refer to it as "the Square." It has a wide boulevard with an island separating the traffic into two lanes with one going north and the other south. The Square is still the most popular shopping area in the city. A proposal has been discussed to make it a pedestrian mall.

There were three movie theatres at the Square, all in walking distance to each other, including the Stanley, Loewe's and the State. The Loewe's was considered the best of the theaters, except I liked the Stanley more. What drew everyone was a songfest before the main feature at the Loewe's was led by an organist. Everyone joined in a sing along as the lyrics were projected on the screen.

It was "corny," but a popular diversion for movie goers that helped to make it a fun date for young high school students. The Stanley was larger than the Loewe's and the State. It had a high ceiling with soft lights that flicked like stars against a dark blue night sky that never interfered with the film. There was nothing special about the State, except it drew large crowds when it showed top films, such as Casablanca, but it has been replaced with retail shops. The Stanley has been restored and is serving another purpose. The Loewe's has withstood any change and was named a National Landmark.

Once, a neighbor asked me if I wanted to see a film at the Square. She was "minding" her brother Jimmy, and I was invited to be his companion. Her boyfriend had a car to drive to the Square. What a break. I was excited when she said the film was at the Loewe's. I could not believe it, but her boyfriend said I needed fifteen cents for a ticket.

Where was I going to get fifteen cents?

I went to ask my mother for the money, but she gave me a nickel. She knew I needed more, but a nickel was all I could get. Mike told me to ask the neighbor's boyfriend for the dime. I doubted he would give it to me, but I followed Mike's suggestion. I told the boyfriend that five cents was all I could get and asked him for the dime. I felt he could spare it, but he was a cheapskate. My going uptown to a movie was hanging in the balance.

"Okay kid, c'mon," he said.

It would have been impolite for me to cheer, but I was tempted and going on my first trip to the Square to see a movie. As we passed his store, I shouted to Mr. Rosen about going to see a movie. He waved, but I was not sure he heard me. I asked the boyfriend to drive around the block, so I could get another chance to tell him about going to the Square.

"Forget it," he said with a surly reply.

"Oh, give the kid a break," my neighbor said.

"Yeah, give me a break," I pleaded

"No way," he said. "You're a dime short and I ain't a taxi service. You're only going to keep the brat company, so shut up."

I was upset, but my neighbor was angry, which led to some bad words between them. Some, I had never heard before. Others I cannot repeat, but once he referred to her as a "bitch."

That was enough for my neighbor.

After he called her a you know what with my neighbour said she was not his girlfriend anymore and wanted to go home, adding a few choice of her own words. Their escalating verbal battle was more serious than I thought. I looked to her brother Jimmy for help, but he just sat there with a dumb look.

What a dope, I thought.

"Aw, honey," the boyfriend said with a moan.

"Yes, you did," she said, continuing to pout.

Their spat was spoiling my chance to see a film. I could understand my neighbor's reaction, but she did not like her boyfriend calling her a "bitch." I bet he called her a lot worse. Fortunately, "the bozo," which is what she called him after he called her a "bitch" kept driving, but both their long silence worried me.

I knew I had to do something.

Mike told me if I wanted a wish to come true, I had to hold my breath, which was a sure way to get what I wanted. Mike always had important information like that to tell me. I took a deep breath, hoping it would work, so I could see my first movie at the Loew's. I held my breath for a long time, wondering who would be the first to say something. Finally, the bozo spoke the magic words.

"Honey, I'm sorry."

Fortunately, she nodded her acceptance to his apology. I liked it more when she called him a bozo, but I knew my wish had come true and let out my breath. It was just in time because I could not have held it any longer. The bozo said he was sorry to call her a bad name. That was okay with me, as long as he kept driving uptown. When she smiled, I knew we were on our way to the Square.

When we reached the Loewe', I was impressed with the lobby. It had a Victorian décor that included gold trimmed columns in the lobby. I kept telling Jimmy what a treat it was to be at the Loew's, except he was still not saying anything. I thought he was a dud, and I was getting tired of him. Between Jimmy and the bozo, I was dealing with a couple of losers and my neighbor didn't help.

"Quiet," she said over my remarks.

"Leave the kid alone, he's excited."

I could not believe the bozo defended me.

What a pair, I thought. They were both losers, arguing again, but it didn't matter. We were going to our seats to see the movie, "Pennies from Heaven." The film was made in Middletown, New Jersey with Bing Crosby in the lead role, singing a popular song with the same title as the movie. I liked the song and Bing Crosby, but not as much as I later liked Frank Sinatra.

The song became one of America's favorites. During intermission the organist played it for a sing along except Jimmy ignored it. It had a simple lyric that was easy to follow. A bouncing ball passed over the lyrics projected on the screen to help the audience. My neighbor and her boyfriend sang it louder than anyone else, except they were off key. On the way home, the boyfriend sang the song again. He sounded awful, so I sang the opening line with a few lyrics I knew.

"Every time it rains, it rains pennies from heaven."

"Hey, the kid isn't bad," the bozo said.

"Yeah, sing some more," my neighbor urged.

"Every time it rains it rains pennies from heaven," I sang, which was all I knew.

"That's enough, the bozo said. You don't want to overdo a good thing," "except when it comes to you, babe."

Oh, brother, did this guy have a line.

I wondered what my neighbor saw in him. I thought she could do better than what he offered, but when she giggled over his dumb remark I wasn't sure about her, either. I was too young to be interested in girls, except if they were pretty the way they were in the movies, but I thought she did not have much to interest anyone.

It did not matter any longer. We reached Bright Street and my day at the movies was over. I was glad I would not have to spend any more time with Jimmy or listen to my neighbor's arguments with her boy friend. At least, I saw a film at the Square for a nickel.

"Hey kid," the bozo called me. "Next time, don't forget to bring the fifteen cents to see a movie at the Square. I'm not a bank for you to go to the movie."

"Yeah, sure," I said.

I would never go to the movies with him again, I said as I hurried to tell my parents about my excursion. Mostly, I wanted to sing the song from the movie at least the one line I knew.

Telling my parents about what happened between my neighbor and her boyfriend was the best part of going uptown to see a movie, especially the part where he called her a "bitch" and she called him a "bozo." My paents could not stop laughing and wanted to hear about it again and again.

I had to repeat the event several times.

Later, Pete and I went to the movies together. Our favourites were epic films with pirate ships and duelling, but our interests changed when we saw the "Andy Hardy" films with Mickey Rooney. We were envious of everything about him. He was a teenager, who lived in a big house on a pretty street in a nice town. He had a car, even if it was a "jalopy," as well as a steady girlfriend.

In one of his films, he had an after school job at a garage, where he was able to repair his car with the help of a mechanic. When he got in a jam, his father patiently bailed him out of trouble with a mild lecture. What a break he had. We had to get out of our jams. We liked everything about the Andy Hardy film, but felt if it was not a movie role he would have been one lucky guy.

We had moved from Bright Street closer to the Square. Pete and I were going to movies there to see films on Saturday afternoons, when there were a lot of empty seats. At least, I didn't have to double up two to a seat and made myself comfortable.

Mickey Rooney was great as Andy Hardy, but he did not interest us, except for the girls he dated. We were interested in the role of his father in the series, old Judge Hardy, played by Lewis Stone. We thought his performance was an acting gem. He was patient and went to work in a suit and tie, which was the way we wanted to dress on a job, not used work clothes as my father did. Pete said we had to work in an office to dress up as they did in the film.

After seeing the Andy Hardy films, we had a respect for what my father did working at an oil refinery. The country soon faced a new threat. The German dictator, Adolph Hitler was at war with Britain and France, but we kept dancing and going to the movies. Of all things, Japan made a surprise attack on Pearl Harbor in Oahu, Hawaii. President Roosevelt declared an immediate state of war against Japan. A day later Germany became an ally of Japan and declared war on the U.S. We were forced to fight two wars, one in Europe and the other in the Pacific.

It was not long before we saw men in uniform throughout the city. Small flags were displayed in home windows with a blue star to signify someone was in the armed services. Later, a new flag appeared with a gold star, which meant a serviceman in the family had been killed in action.

World War II became more difficult than the Depression. It was a harsh change, but everyone approved the prompt decisions against Germany and Japan. President Roosevelt promised our ultimate victory. It would be difficult with both so far away, but the nation was supportive. Early in April, 1942, an aerial attack everyone hopped would succeed was made by the U.S. Army Air Force with the aid of the U.S. Navy in a bombing raid on Tokyo, Japan. It was an incredible mission, as was the invasion of occupied France that led to the over throw of Germany. It was serious, but America began expanding again after a major bombing raid.

19

A Gin Brewing Adventure

The law banning the sale of liquor had been active for a decade, but the Depression was still dominating the economy in a downward spiral. It was 1932 with a national election only several months away. The edict opposed to liquor had worn thin on voter attitudes and America wanted Franklin D. Roosevelt elected president as much as it wanted Prohibition repealed.

A great deal of gin was being brewed in bathtubs to satisfy local demand, many by unemployed young amateurs. The prospect did not escape Mike. He was despondent over not having a job and felt the money he would make brewing gin would be better than no job at all, except it would not be a frivolous endeavour.

Mike said it started when several men came to Bright Street looking for volunteers to brew gin. They knew enough to go to the Knights of Columbus, where young men gathered in the evening to discuss where they might get a job. It was never productive, but it proved to be a good move for the recruiters.

Joey Hallon, a friend of Mike, said he was ready to join the venture, if Mike was interested. A meeting was set up that Mike said was more like a casual get together than a business discussion, but it didn't take long for a deal to be completed. Mike discussed the project with John, who had a job and did not want to get involved. He said Prohibition was "doomed."

For Mike it was an "iffy" deal and had his doubts, but decided to go ahead and brew gin. Two other young men joined the team. One was a friend of Mike named Shutz he called "Shultie" and Tony Mezzo from the downtown area. Mike felt good to have them, but "Shultie" also had a car. It was the clincher Mike needed. What was important was the identity of the men who came looking for volunteers to brew gin.

One was Phil Compton, who said it was a made up name. He worked as an aide for a liquor distributor with another alias called "Mickey the Bull" that he liked. Phil handled it as a variety of assignments. Primarily, he was Mickey's driver, but also active finding young men to brew gin during Prohibition. Liquor was smuggled to Red Bank on the Jersey Shore to make it easy to deliver liquor to New York, but Phil saw to it that he got his share for Mickey's customers, not speakeasies, but personal clients. There were few of them.

My brother Mike in the 1930's when he rode the
rails" later when he fought as a prize fighter.

No one knew Mickey's real name, but he liked being referred to as "the Bull," another alias. He told everyone he was born here, but the scuttlebutt was he arrived in America with his parents, when he was two years old. With his size and physical appearance, he was not hard to identify. He had olive skin, bad teeth, black hair and eyes and a balding scalp. He also had a broken nose that was flattened in a street fight. John said everyone who met him was quick to say his presence matched his forbidding personality.

He spoke softly and dressed in expensive clothes, except his threatening reputation was the type no one wanted to oppose. People where he grew up said his only vice was to smoke Cuban cigars, but he gnawed on the ends until they were only stubs that created a bad breathe.

He did not drink, but loved to eat clams on the half shell at a street food stand that he topped off with a cup of lemon ice, which helped to promote his image as a regular guy, but his reputation convinced everyone to be wary of him.

Mike said his history was mixed with rumoes. His first job was supposedly on the docks, where he was a shape up boss selecting work crews to load and unload cargo ships. The process was rife with partiality, but the workers were afraid to complain. One day, he was not managing shape up work on the docks anymore, but directing a street "numbers game." It was a penny ante racket that was the only kind of gambling low paid workers could afford, but it did not interest Mickey.

He loved the challenge of delivering liquor. It was an approved business to him, especially when he measured the profits. Why not? He did little of the work and took none of the risks. He also felt it was patriotic because the American public wanted to drink liquor and he was one of their providers.

Phil soon developed a close association with Mickey. He was in his twenties, half Mickey's age, as well as tall, suave and good looking with a ready smile. He was a snappy dresser, except he also had an impatience that matched Mickey's manner.

Phil's primary task was to soften Mickey's tough guy image. His friendly attitude helped, except he hated doing follow up assignments that made him look like a clerk. He bragged that getting young men to brew gin was a strong example of the qualifications Mickey would like. He had earned a special position working for him.

Mike did not care about Phil's ambition or Mickey's personality. His concern was to find men to brew gin and anxious to get started, but a snag arose when Mickey's friends told him bathtub gin tasted "soapy." Actually, Mike said they were only joking, but Mickey had overreacted to the implication and ordered gin to be brewed using a formula he got to eliminate the problem. It made Mike wish he had never agreed to manage brewing gin, but backing out of a deal was not done on Bright Street.

There are more than several ways to produce gin. All are complicated and none easy, especially to novice brewers. The process starts with grain alcohol, plus the blending of many ingredients that everyone insists cannot be done in a bathtub, at least, not a gin with an agreeable flavor. A large metal vat produced the best product, except for a still. Joey had a vat stored in his basement, so there was not a problem over a soapy bathtub taste Mickey wanted to eliminate.

A myriad number of ingredients are needed to brew gin besides alcohol. There are all kinds of natural products. Coriander seeds diminish the harsh taste of alcohol and Juniper berries give gin its unique flavour. Several unusual ingredients are needed to get the desired taste, such as crushed tree barks, dried orange peels and plant roots. The use of a "still" or small tower to boil off excess product is one of them also necessary, but Mike said it would make brewing gin vulnerable to detection. Joey suggested that they boil the residue outside in large pots.

Ironically, Prohibition curtailed the production of liquor that created the demand for bootleg gin. It was a simple matter of supply and demand. Gin drinkers were willing to make allowances to get a suitable substitute. During Prohibition, when bathtub gin was mixed with a soda, such as a cola, most gin drinkers felt it was good enough. They ignored its harsh taste, but no one used bathtub gin to make a Martini. Only expensive top brand liquor was being smuggled in from Europe, Canada, and

Mexico to the Northeast to make sophisticated drinks for a bevy of anxious clients.

The more Mike reviewed the formula the more he hated the prospect of using it. What was important to brew gin the way Mickey wanted it were the ingredients to do it, appropriately called "flavourings.

There was always a chance to brew a more than adequate gin from the formula, if it was properly implemented, except he was not sure how to do it. The first issue was to get the required flavourings that were not readily available, unless you went to a food specialty store, except there were few in the city. Buying them was also an indication they were being used to brew liquor. Mike wanted to avoid that possibility. He was already concerned too many people knew about the project. His dilemma involved how to use the special ingredients, but was not sure whether to do it in a mass or selectively. No one told him.

"Do you know anything about what Mickey wants in his gin," Mike asked Joey?

"Only Coriander seeds," he said.

"What about them?"

"They're an ingredient in pastrami."

"Are you kidding me," Mike asked?

"No. I learned about them at a deli."

"Coriander seeds are used to make pastrami," Mike repeated in disbelief.

"Yeah," Joey said, in a minor response.

"Tell me a joke," Mike asked laughing.

He was surprised by Joey's comment, but it did not erase his problem. "How could anyone come up with a formula that was used to make pastrami?" He wanted to give up the project, but knew he couldn't do that. He was sorry he ever thought brewing gin would be easy, but he reached a simple decision. If Mickey wanted gin made using his formula, Phil would have to get the ingredients. "We're not making pastrami, we're brewing gin," Mike said in a sarcastic tone. A short time later, he and Joey went to discuss the problem with Phil, who Mike called "the chauffer" with disdain. It would be an important meeting. Mike insisted he could not get any of the ingredients needed in Mickie's formula to brew gin as he wanted.

"We can't make gin the way Mickey wants it without them," Mike said.

"What do you mean, you can't make the gin," Phil asked in a disturbed tone?

Mike thought it was a test question.

"I didn't say, I can't make it," Mike replied. "I just don't know where to get the stuff to do it."

"What stuff?"

"All the seeds and roots we need."

"What the hell do roots have to do with the formula," Phil asked?

His question told Mike what he suspected. Phil knew nothing about brewing gin and less about the ingredients in Mickey's infamous formula.

"Show him the list," Mike told Joey.

"You don't know where to get the stuff," Phil said slowly, checking the list.

"We can't make gin the way Mickey wants it until we get all of them," Mike emphasized.

"Okay, okay," he said. "I'll work on it," but said he hoped Mike knew what he was doing. He made a terse reply for Phil to just get the added ingredients. Later, Phil asked Joey if Mike wanted to get out of the deal.

"No," Joey said, but he did feel Mike might want to abandon the project. Joey made up his mind to ask him about it. He also mentioned Phil's question about Mike giving up the project.

"To hell with Phil," Mike said.

He felt the formula created a problem he had not anticipated. Mike's only hope was that getting the flavourings could not be done. The plan would have to be abandoned and Mike's gin deal would be cancelled, but no such luck. After several days, the ingredients arrived by a special messenger. Mike never knew where they came from and never asked. He knew he would have to brew Mickey's gin with the ingredients, except he was back to his old dilemma. How to do it?

He pondered the problem for several days. Finally, Joey asked him what he was going to do with the stuff in the bags. They were a vital part of the process that was supposed to be immersed in the mixture for varying lengths of time, but Mike felt they only added to keeping him on edge.

"Mickey will have to take what we give him," he said with conviction. Mike took charge to brew gin with a new resolve. He began throwing in different amounts of the ingredients into the tub. In went the Juniper berries and Coriander seeds. Then he added the tree barks and orange peels, as well as the rest of the loose ingredients he would filter out of the final mixture.

"Here they go," he said.

Joey wanted to take over and toss in the roots, but Mike objected. He did not want him to be responsible, if the gin was a flop. After all the flavorings were added, Mike and Joey took turns stirring the mixture, but they let it sit overnight for several days. Finally, they felt no more stirring was needed, but they were too tired to do anymore stirring and began boiling off the remaining mixture.

When Mike felt the brew had been cooked enough, he got a cup to taste a sample. At first, he took a small sip, but then swallowed a big slug of the gin. He waited a minute then banged the oar he used to stir the mixture on top of the metal tub that produced a loud bang.

"Is it okay," Joey asked, excited?

"Oh, yeah," Mike said.

He did not know how it happened, but his random brewing of the gin mixture worked. Maybe Mickey had the right idea with the formula. The brew had a clear color with a pleasant odor and appealing taste most bathtub gins don't have. Mike's brewing, had a slight, nutty flavour most good gins have from the brewing of the right ingredients in the right way.

At best, gin brewed in a bathtub usually has an amber color with a heavy odor and harsh taste, but the flavor helped eliminate the problem. If he had to do it again, Mike said he was ready, but felt it was only dumb luck for the Gin to turn out so good.

The real test came when Mike asked our father to try the gin. He was a rye whiskey drinker, but Mike felt he would be the best judge of the gin, except he objected to being a guinea pig. Mike told him how carefully it had been brewed. Finally, he won Pop over, who agreed to taste the gin. They hurried to the bathtub brewery in the basement of Joey's small house, where Mike had put a metal tub.

My father took a swig of gin then a gulp. Mike and Joey awaited his verdict. He said it tasted good, without excitement. There was mo burn when he swallowed the gin and smoother than the rye whiskey he drank. Mike was surprised his appraisal was so subdued, but he was satisfied. He expected to hear a more exuberant testimonial, but clapped his hands thinking about the money he was going to make.

He wanted to dance around the tub, as he did before. It was a time for them to celebrate. Joey did it instead, but without banging the oar on the tub. Mike's next move was to meet, Phil. It took several days, but a meeting was set up. Mike put a sample of the gin in a milk bottle and went to meet him. He was in the Packard he drove for Mickey. It was Phil's office. Mike smiled when he saw it in the shadows across the street that made it hard to see inside the car.

He approached the Packard slowly. Phil was sitting behind the wheel. Mike went to sit in the back, passing his hand over the smooth upholstery. The car was one of the premier vehicles of the 1930's and he admired it. Joey was nervous, as he slid into the front trying to be confident next to Phil. "Here's the best bathtub gin you'll ever drink," he said laughing, as he got the bottle with gin to pass to Phil. Mike had put it in a brown paper bag to hide its contents, but Phil only turned to look at Joey, without extending his hand.

"Have you tried it," he asked.

"Sure, so did Shultie and Mike's old man."

"Mike's old man"

"How many guys know about it?"

"That's all," Joey said.

"Did you use the flavorings?"

It was a direct question to Mike.

"Sure," he replied.

"Wait till you taste it," Joey said.

Phil looked around all sides of the car. When he was sure no one was watching, he pulled off the leather gloves he used to drive the Packard and laid them in his lap. He reached over to open the car's small storage compartment to remove a silver flask. He took off the top and it became a cup.

He carefully took hold of the milk bottle. His every move was deliberate, as he poured out gin to fill the cup. He sniffed it and took a sip before he swallowed the rest in a quick gulp. He remained silent, but had a pleased look on his face.

"Mickey will love it," he said.

"Great," Mike said with a tinge of sarcasm.

"How much have you made," he asked?

"A tub full," he said, repeating Joey's figure.

"Great. Make three more tubs," he added.

"When do we get paid," Mike asked?

Phil paused to stare at him. His question interrupted the joyous mood, but Phil brought out a money clip and pulled off two twenties. He gave one to Mike and the other to Joey. Mike asked for money for Hank and Tony. Phil took his time, but he gave Mike two fives, saying he would give them more when they delivered the rest of the gin.

"How much," Mike asked.

"A lot more," Phil said.

Mike looked pleased. After the meeting, Phil left them in front of the Knights of Columbus where their gin collaboration began. The next day Mike would get five gallon containers to store the gin and start the brewing process again using Mickey's formula. He was sure it would not be the same, but it would be good enough.

Phil had another mission.

He wanted Mickey to taste the gin sample, as he sped to his apartment, but Mickey would never learn how good a product it was. It was dark without enough light on the streets. Going too fast, Phil ran through an intersection and hit another car crossing in front of him. Phil never had an accident before, but his first was close to being his only one.

He was thrown against his car's windshield and had a severe concussion. Nothing happened to the other driver. He was only shaken from the collision, but the sample bottle of gin spilled over the car seat and the floor. The police quickly called for medical help, but he was also issued a reckless driving charge for driving under the influence of alcohol.

The near tragic event convinced Phil to give up the gin business, but the incident did not end there. It soon took another ironic turn. Mickey was despondent over Phil's accident and collapsed from a heart attack in his apartment. He was incapacitated and forced to give up any kind of work.

The saga of Mike brewing gin ended when Shultie drove him and John to a deserted street with the five gallon containers of gin to pour down a sewer. John said he was glad the project was over. Mike was quick to agree, except he saved several milk bottle samples of gin to give to neighbors.

Brewing gin in a bathtub was no longer a business, but a weekend hobby. In November, 1932, Franklin D. Roosevelt was elected president. The next year Prohibition was repealed and the country was pleased it was over.

It was a ridiculous law.

Many people believed it caused problems that were harder to control, including the growth of illegal gangs. The impact of unemployment continued, but was no longer a major issue. The Depression ended with the build up to a war with Japan and Germany. A popular song the people liked became a reality.

"Happy days are here again."

20

A Football Game

It was a fall Saturday in October when Pete suggested we go to see Paul play football instead of a movie. Everyone in the neighborhood was talking about his exploits on the gridiron for Dickinson High School. It would be my first time to see him play.

Pete said we had to hurry or we would miss the game. Dickinson played at the High School Field, not far from Bright Street, but we wanted to get to the game before it started We ran as fast as we could and only stopped to catch our breath. We didn't have money to see the game, and depended on Paul to get us pass the entrance gate. When we arrived, a crowd was still at the entry gates.

We knew we had reached the field in time and walked along a fence, where Pete said there was an open gate. I was surprised to find it partially open, but a guard commanded who went in and who went out. Luck was with us. Paul was with his team getting ready for pregame warm ups. He persuaded the guard to let us inside to the stand.

"I told you we could do it," Pete said.

I gave him a big smile of approval, as we moved toward the stands, but paused to observe the field and the spectators. It was an average, but exuberant crowd for a high school game. Dickinson's appearance on the field was greeted by a band that began to play a strong marching rendition. What a show. I loved it.

"C'mon," Pete said. "Hurry up."

As we went to the stands to find seats, I saw my father, who was at the game with John. He did not know much about football, but enjoyed seeing Paul play. The fans, primarily students, cheered as the starting players on each team were introduced. I told everyone I was Paul's brother and they cheered me, too. I was going to mention Pete, but that would over doing it. Mostly, I was awed by the size of the players and Paul looked bigger than most of them.

Dickinson was in maroon jerseys with pants of old gold. The opposing team had a more classic look with blue jerseys, white pants and helmets. I told Pete their bulging shoulder pads and leather helmets made the players look fierce.

"That's how they're supposed to look," he said.

Pete and I became ardent football fans and kept going to games to root for Paul, as long as the guard let us in without a ticket. We were also fans of a Navy player named Fred Borries, a running back who scored a lot of touchdowns. His nickname was "Buzz" that fit his image, but seeing Paul play was the start of Pete and I following him in the game.

We did not have a football, but we made one out of an old newspaper. We folded it until it was about eight inches long then rolled it as tight as we could to three inches thick. It was easy to toss forward passes with it to pretend we were football stars. "Look out, I shouted here comes Buzz Borries" with a straight arm pose, after catching Pete's forward pass with our newspaper football.

After making All State at Dickinson, Paul played for Fordham and was a teammate of Vince Lombardi, who became one football's most renowned coaches. Paul was named to Fordham's Hall of Fame, and later starred for the Green Bay Packers.

Pete followed Paul in his football career at Dickinson and started at tackle for three years. He was named All State in his senior year and attended Notre Dame. He played on its 1943 Championship team. Paul and Pete were named together to the Hudson County All Sports Hall of Fame.

It was a special honor.

After his final season at Notre Dame, Pete was drafted by the Detroit Lions, but signed to play with the Los Angles Dons, a team in the newly formed All American Football Conference. He signed for more than the Lions offered. Later, Pete played with the Baltimore Colts, another team in the new League.

I played for Dickinson High School and went to West Virginia, but ended injuring my knee in so that my football career was curtailed. West Virginia is a great university with a stellar School of Journalism, which was the right academic career choice for me.

Paul was physically big and fast, and with his reputation as a strongman his friends were the first to encourage him to play football. He became a standout, but my mother was not a football fan. She thought my father wanted Paul to get a job, but he liked the game and enjoyed the recognition Paul received. His co-workers at the oil refinery often mentioned Paul, adding to my father's pride.

Paul was my mother's favourite. We were surprised by her reaction to football. She always supported what Paul wanted to do, except she said something had to be done to get him to give up football.

My mother remained determined to save him from what she described football as a "bummie" game. When she used her inventive adjective to describe the game was the most derogatory idiom she could have applied. She should have talked to my father about her feelings. I'm sure he would have convinced her to support Paul's playing football.

Dickinson's coach, Charlie Witkowski, who later became the mayor of Jersey City, met my mother at the field to talk with her. Whatever he said alleviated her concerns. Later, she told my father he said Paul was a great player and the team needed him.

He was not surprised. Paul had a strong reputation in football. He smiled at the coach's opinion that was similar to his own. Paul told John he remained composed over my mother's feeling, but several days later he was thinking about quitting football to get a job.

John understood his intent, but urged Paul to continue football, as a means to a college scholarship. It wasn't long before my mother's opposition became an amusing story in the family, and we joked that Charlie Witkowski called to ask if she was ready to help coach the team.

With the turmoil over Paul playing football, my mother went to one of his team's practices. The area was at Boyle's Thirty Acres across the street from the High School Field, where Pete and I saw Paul play. The location was the site of Jack Dempsey's 1921 Championship fight against the French champion, Georges Carpentier more than a decade later.

The fight was a national sports event. Over 50,000 fans were at the match in portable stands erected for the fight. Many celebrities attended the fight, including: John D. Rockefeller Jr., the head of Standard Oil. Henry Ford, the most famous name in the automobile industry. George M. Cohan, the song writer and musical producer. Al Jolson, the Broadway singing star, who was a big sports fan attended the match, as well as the writers H. L. Mencken and Ring Lardner. The fight was a struggle between two strong pugilists, but Dempsey won the bout in the fourth round. For a time, its impact made Jersey City nationally prominent.

21

A Big Boy

My mother said her special feelings toward my brother Paul started when he was born. At twelve pounds, he was the biggest baby in the maternity ward, but his size pleased my parents.

When he was fourteen years old, he was six feet tall with broad shoulders and a large torso. At sixteen, he was six feet two inches and 210 pounds, which was big for a teenager in the 1930's.

His record as a standout athlete was more than matched by his rating in academics, especially in the sciences of math, physics and chemistry. His bookish nature made him a favourite of his teachers, as well as a regular visitor to the office of the school's principal, Dr. Frank McMackin, who wrote math textbooks. Paul would try to stump him with problems he created. They could be heard laughing in his office as they discussed solutions, but there was always a question of who was having the most fun the student or the teacher.

In addition to keeping up with his studies, he followed a strict body building regimen. Despite his physical size, he was an accomplished gymnast. It was a startling sight to see his huge frame perform on the parallel bars, as well as doing giant swings on the high bar. He was also into weight lifting, which gave him a dominate physique.

He had a narrow waist, huge biceps and muscular thighs that earned him a reputation as a strongman. A common sight in the morning was to see him walk to the bathroom on his hands, but at the gym he also did handstands on a table then dropped to the floor without losing his excellent form. It was called an impossible feat.

In addition to his physical workouts, he kept trying new exercises. He used a solid iron bar that stood five feet high, and three inches thick that weighed over a hundred pounds. He would lift it over his head to develop his upper arm and shoulder strength. His most challenging exercise was to stand up the end of bar and grasp it at the top with one hand, as he lifted it straight up several feet, but kept his arm extended and unbent. A lot of his friends tried to do it, but no one could duplicate the feat.

Despite his weight lifting, his most versatile activity may have been as a swimmer. Neighbors on Bright Street said he was born to the water and called him a "human fish." I was five years old when he first took me swimming at the Gap. Good swimmers leaped into the water from a pier. I had not learned how to swim and used the ladder to go down to Paul, waiting for me in the water. He lifted me onto his back with one arm as I straddled my legs around his waist, as best I could, then he swam out into the river. New York's skyscrapers created an incredible scene with tugboats tooting their horns to warn us of their presence, but Paul kept us at a safe distance. I enjoyed being with him on my water adventures and waved to the men on tugboats, who always waved back.

With Paul's help, Pete passed his first swimming test without an inner tube. He was on the pier when Paul yanked it from him and in the best tradition of the older brother teaching his sibling how to swim he tossed Pete into the water. At first, he was out of sight, but then he burst out of the water gasping for air, flaying his arms, wishing he had his tube.

"Swim," Paul shouted to him.

He quickly responded with strong arm strokes, as he swam to the dock and out again, stopping only to tread water. I never understood how it worked, but the test proved Pete did not need his inner tube anymore. I was glad I never had to learn how to swim by the sink or swim method, but it worked for Pete.

We had many thrills at the Gap, but the most exciting time was watching Paul and his friend Steve Chevanski do daredevil dives from the top of a 30 foot high crane. They would climb nearly to the top, and like Mexican cliff divers they did dramatic swan dives into the water sometimes in tandem.

Watching them on hot summer evenings was a special event to residents on Bright Street. Neighbors who never went to the Gap would line the dock. I often went with my father to watch Paul and Steve perform, as thrilled as anyone in the crowd.

In all his athletic efforts, Paul was a standout in football, but the cheers diving at the Gap came from fans at his high school football games. Today, there are many examples of players from various backgrounds going to college on a "free ride" after displaying their skills to play football.

Few became rich playing professional football in the 1930's, as they do today, but it had a different purpose for Paul. He wanted more, so much more. He knew that football could provide a college scholarship, especially with his "A plus" test record in high school. It would not be easy, but it would enable him to go to college to study premed and chemistry to qualify for medical school.

Paul wanted to be a doctor.

In the 1930's, less than 5 per cent of American adults had a college degree. The figure reached 20 per cent in 1950 following World War II, thanks to the G.I. Bill, a government plan that helped pay college costs for veterans. Today, the number of college graduates is estimated at 23 per cent, male and female, but some analysts challenge the figure, saying it is close to 30 per cent. With the emphasis on education, the number is sure to grow, but the rising cost of college can leave graduates deeply in debt. The threat of attacks on college students with automatic guns needed the government to correct both the gun threats and their costs.

A former Jersey City judge, Ezra Nolan, a big Dickinson football fan, was sure Paul would be offered a college scholarship to play football. Several neighbors challenged the prospect. It was a desperate time, especially for the son of a blue collar immigrant. A college degree counts for so much today, but in the 1930's the plan to attend college was rife with what if questions.

The fears of the Depression created a different attitude. Most families could not afford the cost of college, reasonable as they were compared to today's costs. Some applicants could not meet the required grade point average. The conviction was to learn a trade and get a steady job, which was promoted by many sources and may have once again opened a route to jobs.

My father never felt one of his children would go to college and knew of no one's son or daughter who did. He was proud of Paul's accomplishments and felt that a college education must be important, except for the effect the dismal economy had on his thinking. He wondered if a college was worth it with few jobs available.

It was a reasonable concern.

The question was mired in a lifestyle that had him labor at a level just above poverty. His reaction might have been different, if the Depression did not have such a negative effect on the economy. With so many out of work, most people felt that a high school education was sufficient to learn a trade and make a living.

Several of my father's friends said Paul could get a job at the refinery where he worked and build his way up to a position of a foreman. That prospect excited my father, except Paul was not interested in working at an oil refinery.

He wanted to study medicine to be a doctor.

Paul's goal concerned my father. America was changing too fast for him to keep up with changing attitudes. He only wanted what was best for his son. The choice was Paul's, but was he right? He knew a scholarship was the assurance for him to go to college. Was it a real possibility, my father wondered? Could Paul become a doctor? Was it possible to reach for the stars?

Was it possible?

One fact was certain. My father could not pay for a college education or a medical degree. To resolve his dilemma, he turned to where he always went when he faced a difficult decision. He asked John what should be done. It was a role reversal between father and son. John said there was no option. Paul had to go to college, but a resolution on medical school could wait. A short time later, an unrelated event would support John's opinion.

It was 9:00 PM on a warm Indian summer night in October, 1934. The night was cool, but comfortable with no hint of what was going to occur. Paul's high school football team was scheduled to play a game the next day against a cross town rival. My parents and I were leaving the front room to get ready for bed when we were surprised by a loud voice that came up from the street below.

"Where does Paul Berezney live?"

"In the tenement on the second floor."

"Paul, Paul," the shouts rose from the crowd, as we hurried to our front room window. I was next to Paul with my father leaning over my shoulder. We quickly learned that students from his high school had gathered to cheer him at a rally before the next day's game.

"Tell those bums to go away," my mother said.

"They're not bums. They're from my school."

I saw Pete in the crowd and called to him, but a band paraded around the corner playing a marching tune with a drum beat that kept him from hearing me.

"They want Paul," he shouted.

"We know," I shouted back.

The crowd continued to grow larger. It wasn't long before it filled the area in front of our tenement, as well as the school across the street, where a light illuminated the scene. It was a festive crowd still gathering below us. By now, it stretched almost to the corner to the left, where there was another street light. Bright Street looked like a Hollywood film setting. A group had also gathered in the shadows to the right, content to be a part of the exuberant music and cheers from the crowd. All the while the chant for Paul grew louder. Everyone was clapping, as the band played the school's rousing fight song. I wanted to join the festivities, but my mother would not let me, except most of our neighbours came out to join the crowd.

John and Mike were not home. I was sure they would have liked to have seen the spectacle. Rallies for a college football game are a common scene today, but not for a high school game in the 1930's. Paul dressed and went down to join the crowd. When he appeared a fast drum roll sounded that ended with a clash of cymbals.

"Paul, Paul, Paul," the crowd cheered, as I did once from our front room window. When he promised a victory in Saturday's game, the cheers exploded. I looked at my father and saw his pleased expression. Several other players took turns addressing the crowd, and finally it was over and the crowd dispersed. The rally occurred long before TV and no radio station knew about the event. Since few people downtown owned a radio, it would not have mattered. It was also too late for a story in the morning newspapers, but Mr. Rosen summed up the event with an appropriate comment. "It was unbelievable," he said, which was a strong summation for a high school football rally. Today, it would be described as a "happening." I thought it was a wonderful event.

The crowd of students left more excited than when they arrived. I could hear the band playing a marching rendition as it rounded the corner away from Bright Street. Pete said he heard a report a policeman made from one of several patrol cars that came to check on the event. He estimated the crowd at close to a thousand, mostly high school students. Mr. Rosen agreed, including neighborhood residents who had joined the crowd.

Looking back, I think Mr. Rosen's estimate was accurate. I have attended many high school and college football rallies since that night. Colleges have larger crowds, but none I saw compared to the excitement of the one on Bright Street in the 1930's. It

over whelmed my mother and father, but the event settled an important question. My parents said nothing was more important than for Paul to get a college education.

It would soon become a reality.

22

The Seven Blocks of Granite

After Paul's senior year in high school, my father was overwhelmed by the number of colleges offering him a football scholarship, as Judge Nolan predicted. Prominent among the list was Rutgers, Columbia, Colgate, New York University, Fordham and Penn State, but the most appealing offer came from the U.S. Naval Academy. It would require a Congressional appointment, but Paul's academic record made him a strong prospect.

The opportunity to go to the Naval Academy excited my father, especially with a Navy Commander in our kitchen to explain the benefits of the Academy. With his achievement as an A-plus student, Paul was assured a lifetime career, easing my father's concern to have a steady job, and what a job. Paul had a strong interest in the Naval Academy, but Ed Franco, a high school teammate, who would be an All American at Fordham had completed his freshman year and was urging Paul to join him at the University.

In the 1930's, Fordham was an Eastern football power. Jim Crowley, one of Notre Dame's Four Horsemen was the head coach. After a meeting with Frank Leahy, one of the team's line coaches, Paul was convinced Fordham was the place for him. Leahy became his close mentor. Later at Notre Dame he was cited as a renowned coach.

Fordham is located in the Bronx, New York in an area called Rose Hill. The campus has a pleasant environment with an enrolment of top rated college students. Outside its gates, there is a busy city. It's of no surprise, but before the University was established, the area was farmland.

Its campus is as it was in the 1930's with a wide lawn or "quad" common to most colleges. Far from isolated the school was close to an elevated train that suited Paul. After all, he was city bred and knew how to travel in an active metropolis.

Paul had a football scholarship, but his academic curriculum was important. He became an active member of the Chemistry and Physics Clubs, highly rated students. Paul was referred to as the best science student at Fordham and admired for participating in the club

Paul before Pittsburgh game in 1937

Picture from Fordham's Sports Information.

One problem prevented his career at Fordham from being fulfilled. He was absorbed in chemistry lab that made him late for practice, but it was impossible for him to leave an unfinished experiment. He was torn between his commitment to football and his love of science, which was common knowledge, as the caption in his college yearbook confirms:

"Paul was known as the mad scientist for every free moment found him working in the chemistry lab. His interest in the sciences often proved irking to Coach Jim Crowley when Paul was late for practice due to some lab work. His feats on the gridiron are known to all, but only Fordham men know the studious and friendly Paul."

He was committed to football, but he did not want to sacrifice his studies in the sciences. After he was detained for practice by a lab test, he knew Jim Crowley would be upset. He regretted his delays of football practice and apologized, but Crowley was unmoved and only nodded.

Paul was referred to as one of Fordham's "promising players," but said he was far ahead of that rating. He felt he was a prominent member of the Fordham line on offense and defense. His ability did not escape his assistant football coaches, especially Frank Leahy, who said "he was outstanding and a top notch performer. In the 1930's, Fordham's football record rivalled most colleges in prominence with some of the country's best linemen. In 1935, Paul's freshman year, Fordham played a 0-0 game against Pittsburgh, a perennial Eastern football power.

The next season the 1936 Pittsburgh game ended in another scoreless tie. After the game, a stalwart defence by Fordham prompted a special reference by Grantland Rice, a renowned sports writer, who had named Notre Dame's 1924 backfield the "Four Horsemen." In his report on the Fordham game with Pittsburgh, he wrote: "The Fordham wall still stands."

Tim Cohane, Fordham's Sports Information Director, a close friend of Paul, who later became the Sports Editor of *Look*, a famous weekly magazine, was searching for a more compelling phrase to describe the team's outstanding line play. He wanted to capture the nation's attention, but felt Rice's accolade lacked the impact. He adopted a slogan used to describe a Fordham team of the 1920's.

The phrase was: The Seven Blocks of Granite.

It caught on imediately, except some of the luster of its 1936 season was tarnished when Fordham was tied by Georgia 7-7 and lost to NYU, 7—6 in an astounding upset. That loss cost Fordham a Rose Bowl invitation that Pittsburgh accepted. After beating the Washington Huskies in the Rose Bowl game, Pittsburgh was assured the number one college ranking.

So who were the players that earned Fordham a famous football reference? According to an article by

Jack Newcomb in a 1940 issue of *SAGA,* a national men's magazine, it took ten players over two seasons to produce the defensive record of the Fordham Rams. After the 1936 season, three linemen graduated. They included the guards, Vince Lombardi and Nat Pierce, and one of its ends, Leo Pacguin. In 1937, the New York sports corps reported the Fordham line was better than its 1936 team and continued to apply the name the Seven Blocks of Granite to its players.

The article of the stated stated:

> *"Because they spanned two seasons, the Seven Blocks of Granite were really ten in number. In 1936, the players included Alex Wojiechowitz at Center, Vince Lombardi and Nat Pierce at guards, Al Barbarsky and Ed Franco at the tackles and Leon Pacquin and Johnny Druze at ends. In 1937, after Nat Pierce, Vince Lombardi and Leon Pacquin graduated, Paul Berezney was at one of the tackles in 1937 with Mike Kochel at guard and Harry Jacunski at end. All these players have clear credentials to membership in the "Seven" Blocks of Granite Club."*

The ten players were all a part of the Seven Blocks of Granite, but according to a book, *Fordham: A History and a Memoir,"* by the Reverend Raymond A. Schroth S.J. He was a Fordham professor, there were not ten, but twelve players who contributed to the success of Fordham's football program. He wrote: "Besides Paul

Berezney, Harry Jacunski and Mike Kochel, the Seven Blocks of Granite also included Jim Hayes and Joe Bernard." They all merit recognition, but the exclusive ten were the famous line led by Paul in 1937.

Sports events were not limited to baseball or football to provide a needed relief from the economy's bad news during the decade. Fordham's football record was only a part of that history.

Several major prize fighting events also took plac during that era, including James J. Braddock's upset of Max Baer for the heavyweight title. Germany's Max Schmelling also beat Braddock in a prize fight that created a rematch of the heavy weight title ot Schmelling against Joe Louis, who won the fight in the first round to regain the crown.

Some people feel that when "Sea Biscuit," a diminutive horse beat "War Admiral" in a match race it was the primary sports event of the year that electrified the country. The New York Yankees made their year a record in baseball with four successive Championships led by Joe DiMaggio and Lou Gehrig. In a presentation at Yankee Stadium with Babe Ruth. Gehrig said he had to give up baseball because of MLS, a serious illinness that caused his death.

Lastly, at the 1936 Olympics in Berlin, Jesse Owens, a black American, won five gold medals in tract. Adolph Hitler was so irate over his performance that dominated Nazi Germany's tract stars caused Hitler to storm out of the stadium.

Many writers have called the 1930's the second Golden Age of Sports. To add to its history, Fordham was preparing to play a historic football game against Pittsburgh to break their 0-0 games. Eastern college football needed the impact of the 1937 event between the two powerhouse teams.

Both teams won their first two games to heighten interest in their upcoming meeting. Following two previous tie games, Fordham was primed for their scuffle as were college sports fans. It was a wait of high anticipation in the North East. Paul was among the players looking forward to the game.

Sports experts predicted it would be a game for the ages and expectations were high for both teams. An extensive radio hook up would broadcast the game. It was a test of Pittsburgh's offense against Fordham's defence. Pittsburgh's backfield made their team the favourite, but Fordham was determined to stop them. It seemed the entire country was waiting for the game, not just fans from the North East. Paul was anxious. The New York Times headline on a pregame report stated:

Franco Shifted to Guard, Change Made to Provide a Starting Berth for Berezney against Pitt

Sports history is often reduced to nothing more than statistics, but the game was destined to become a classic that either team could have won. Celebrities packed the stands. Boxing's former heavyweight champion, Jack

Dempsey, wished Fordham good luck before it took the field. Pittsburgh was rated the solid favourite, despite playing away from home. It had the All-American halfback, Marshall Goldberg, who was a constant threat.

Fordham was confident it had the defensive line to stop him. A touchdown in the game by Pitt was disallowed by a holding penalty. Pittsburgh fans bemoaned its bad luck, but Fordham had its own heartbreak. Its right end, Johnny Druze, the Fordham captain and extra point kicker, missed three field goals. He told me one was an easy attempt he should have made, but the game ended in a 0-0 tie for the third consecutive year. The New York Times headline on the game stated:

Fordham and Pitt Failef to Score for theThird Year, Both Teams Powerful on Defencse

The disappointment was replaced with a positive appraisal of the game that became a part of sports history. The next year Pittsburgh beat Fordham, 24-13. Fordham was leading 7-3 until the fourth quarter, when Paul was injured and had to leave the game. Mike Kochel, a guard, and Ray Riddick, an end were also injured. After that, Marshall Goldberg had an easy time against an undermanned Fordham line.

The Pittsburgh newspaper reported:

"Berezney not only held up the left side of the Fordham line, but the right side as well," adding that Jock Sutherland, the Pittsburgh coach, called his play "outstanding."

Paul was disappointed over the loss. He said a win would have assured the recognition of Fordham as a national power, especially after going undefeated in its other games. Marshall Goldberg selected Paul to his All Opponent team that was published in national newspapers.

It was a special recognition.

When Jock Sutherland was named to coach the Eastern College All Stars against the New York Giants in a charity game, he chose Paul as one of his tackles. Some of the players included: Sid Luckman, a forward passer from Columbia, Marshall Goldberg, a running back from Pittsburgh and Brud Holland, a speedy end from Cornell. They were among the top players in Eastern college football.

An interesting promotional event occurred before the game when Paul and Brud Holland, a track star, ran a forty yard race as an item for the press to see who was the fastest. Speed was one of Paul's strong assets, but no one thought he would beat Holland. He did, but only by a half step.

Paul said Brud Holland lost on purpose. After a business career, Holland, a black American, was named U.S. Ambassador to Sweden. Some of the Seven Blocks players went on to play professional football. A number of them became college coaches. Harry Jacunski played with the Green Bay Packers, but later was an assistant coach at Yale. Frank Leahy led Boston College before he was named to coach Notre Dame. Johnny Druze joined him as one of his chief assistants, as did Harry Jacunski.

Alex Wojiechowski was renowned at Fordham as a center and linebacker. He played with the Detroit Lions, and was one of the top players in the NFL. After playing professional football, Ed Franco, returned to Fordham as one of its coaches. Al Barbartsky changed his name to Bart and played professional football.

Following coaching stints at high schools and in college, Vince Lombardi was named the offensive coach of the New York Giants, but left to be the head coach of the Green Bay Packers, where he produced a record as one of the most respected leaders in football. Meanwhile, Paul followed his dream and enrolled in medical school to become a doctor, but also played tackle for the Green Bay Packers.

Violent Medico

Paul, left, preparing an experiment in the chemistry lab at Marquette Medical School with another future doctor. The picture was taken before his final season.

After graduating from college, Paul enrolled at Marquette Medical School in Milwaukee. He married after his first year at Marquette. A year later his first child was born. He had to support a family, as well as to pay for his medical education. With no recourse than to play football, he signed with the Green Bay Packers in 1942. He kept up his medical studies with an agreement to miss some practices, but was ready to play on Sunday.

Doctors are amazed he was able to attend medical school and play football, but they are also surprised he was only paid $3,000 to do it. It was a meager sum compared to today's salaries, but it was the going rate for top linemen in 1942. With the help of a bank loan, he was able to meet expenses and pay his medical school bills. Following his second season at Marquette he graduated with a degree as a doctor.

Green Bay had strong prospects for the 1944 season with players, such as Don Hutson, the record setting receiver from Alabama and Irv Comp a passing halfback from St. Benedict's College in Kansas,

FRANK LEAHY
DIRECTOR OF ATHLETICS

March 20, 1941.

Mr. Paul Berezney,
Marquette University Medical School,
Milwaukee, Wisconsin.

Dear Paul:

Your letter of February 15th was a real
source of happiness. Needless to say, the sender of
this letter was mighty glad to learn that you are
still pursuing your medical course. There is no
reason in the world why you shouldn't achieve great
success in that field.

If ever there is any little service we can
render you from here, don't hesitate to let us know.
Should you need a little extra cash to finish your
schooling, I will be more than happy to lend a helping
hand. Don't hesitate to call upon me, Paul, if you
need assistance, for I shall welcome an opportunity
to reciprocate in full for what you have done for
Fordham and me.

Best of luck and kind regards,

F. Leahy
FRANK LEAHY

The Green Bay coach was Earl "Curly" Lambeau, one of the founders of the Packers, who was one of established men who started professional football. The Green Bay stadium is named after him. As a coach, he was an experienced strategist and a tough taskmaster, but he also had a considerate manner that earned him the respect of his players. He felt the 1944 Packers had more than a chance to win their division, but he wanted Paul to play right tackle.

Football was still a means to an end for him, but he needed the money. He was in his late twenties with another child in the family, his second daughter, and an internship to complete. Curley Lambeau knew of his financial needs and encouraged him to play one more season. After several phone conferences, he agreed to a contract for $3,500.

In 1944, players played both offense and defense, which added to the physical demands of the game. The Associated Press asked Lambeau if Paul would be in shape to play football. He said he was always working out and was counting on him to be ready.

Lambeau added that he was sending Paul plays in the mail. The Associated Press liked the angle and put it on its national wire. The item became a popular news item, but Paul was amused. He said the plays were the same with few changes, and Lambeau was only having fun with the press.

At the time, the road to the National Football League's Western Division title went through Chicago.

The 1944 season was no exception. The Packers won their opening game, but were scheduled to play the Bears the following week. Chicago still had most of its players from its 1941 and 1943 Championship teams.

The 1944 Bears were said to be equally strong with Sid Luckman the All Pro quarterback directing their offense. At a team meeting several days before their game, Lambeau asked Paul if he was ready to stop the Bears. To emphasize his response, he gave Paul a jab to the stomach. Paul said it reminded him he was still only a football lineman, despite his degree as a doctor.

The game was in Green Bay on a hot Sunday in September. The temperature was 90 degrees, but near a 100 degrees on the field. Everyone said it would have been hotter in Chicago. The Packers built an early lead, but despite a Bears strong comeback. Green Bay won, 42-28. Paul played almost the entire game. That night he had a light dinner, reviewed some medical journals and slept ten hours.

When the Packers traveled to New York to play the Giants at the end of November, Green Bay needed a win or a Bear's loss to clinch the Western Division title, but the Giants were also in pursuit of the Eastern Division crown. Green Bay lost to the Giants, but the Bears also lost, which made the Packers record better than the Bears and the Division winners.

After the game, Paul came home, except there was no crowd to cheer him the way there was years before at a high school rally. A decade had passed with his life filled with family needs after completing his medical degree. Paul strained his left knee in the Giants game, and strurled after one of my mother's special meals, he struggled to bed. It was a joyful but difficult night for a football hero who was now a doctor.

Several years before, Paul made a visit home to see our parents over the holidays. The Bears were in New York to play the National Football League All-Stars in a charity game the league promoted. The game would follow the Bears 73-0 championship victory over the Washington Redskins, one of football's most astounding games. Paul knew Sid Luckman, the Bears' great quarterback from Columbia, when he was at Fordham. They were also teammates on the Eastern College All-Stars. Paul asked me if I would like to go to New York to meet the Bears' players.

Would I?

A few days later, we were up early to leave for the Polo Grounds, where the Bears were practicing. It was early January and a light rain was falling, but it was not cold. The subway exit led up a long flight of stairs to the street, where the stadium's bleachers angled overhead. The Bears were doing walk through drills under the shelter to avoid the light rain.

Paul approached two players leaning over a railing to have their picture taken for a sports reporter. Paul nudged one of them from behind with a gentle poke in the ribs that caused him to turn quickly to see who had interrupted his photo session.

"Paul, you son of a gun," he said.

They hugged and Paul introduced me to Sid Luckman, one of my football heroes. He was one of the first T-Formation quarterbacks, and I later saw him throw seven touchdown passes in a game against the Giants. He introduced Paul to George MacAfee, the premier running back from Duke, who was posing with him for the picture.

Norm Stanley, the Bear's All-Pro fullback from Stanford, came over to do some friendly kidding of Luckman, as well as to greet Paul. The introductions continued, including: Clyde "Bulldog" Turner, the All Pro center from Harden-Simmons, Danny Fortman, the Bears' guard and captain from Colgate. Bill Osmanski, a halfback from Holy Cross, who played with Paul on the College All Stars, and Johnny Siegal, Luckman's pass catching teammate at Columbia.

They were all professional football stars. I could not have been more excited. It would be similar to be introduced to Tom Brady and the Patriot players. After the Bears finished their walk through drills, Luckman introduced Paul to George Halas, the coach and founder of the Chicago Bears.

"This is Paul's young brother, Steve," he said.

"How are you doing," Mr. Halas asked me?

How was I doing?

I was usually talkative, but I could not say a word. I felt he understood my awed silence. He put his arm around my shoulder, as we headed to the locker room.

"I'm doing fine," I said.

"What," Mr. Halas asked?

"You asked me how I was doing. I'm fine."

"Good," Mr. Halas replied laughing

George Halas was already a legend, and I appreciated his patience. He had a reputation as a tough coach and a tougher owner, but he seemed to be a pleasant man. In the locker room, Paul discussed playing for the Bears with Mr. Halas. It sounded settled to me. Somehow, he signed to play with the Green Bay Packers instead and preparing to play the Giants for the championship.

After their previous game, the Giants and Packers played two games before their meeting for the title at the Polo Grounds, a field Paul knew from his playing days at Fordham. I only hoped his injured knee would not hinder him. It was mid December 1944, and the people who cared for him the most were in place for the event.

John was at the stadium with my parents, while Mike was there with Pat, his brother in law. Pete was at Notre Dame and would listen to the game on the radio, while Paul's wife and children would do the same in Wisconsin.

The 1944 Green Bay Packers

Team picture is of the Green Bay Packers before the start of its Championship season. Paul is in the top row the third from the left after Earl Lambeau, the coach and Don Hutson.

John and Mike saw Paul play in college. I only went to a few of his college games, but Demie and I went to see him when the Packers came to New York. After our football game on Saturday, we would meet him where he was staying. Paul would pay for a sumptuous dinner, get us a room and sideline passes to sit on the bench for the game. The next day at school, we bragged about the day to our friends.

For the championship, the Packers spent the week before the game in Charlottesville, Virginia to escape inclement weather and hold private practices. The team arrived in New York on Saturday night, but that was too late for us to meet him. Early Sunday morning, we went to the Hotel Commodore next to Grand Central Station, where the team was staying. It is now the Grand Hyatt Hotel. The lobby was abuzz with reporters, who were always present before a big sports event.

A discussion about the NFL Championship game could be heard throughout the lobby, but for the first time, I thought Paul was not in his usual casual mood, not nervous, but determined. The winning share for the game would be $1,500 per player, almost half his salary. It was a lot of money to make to play a football game in 1944. There were many reporters throughout the lobby who wanted to talk with the players. One came over to wish Paul good luck. He was cordial and spoke openly of his support.

I heard another reporter make a startling statement to a group in the lobby. "As Paul Berezney goes so goes the Packer's line," he said. It was an adaption of an old sports cliché, but in a way, it was a compliment, except being laden with responsibility. I hoped Paul would fulfill the prediction. He had been performing at an outstanding level all season, but this game would be more demanding.

Playing on their home field, the Giants were a seven point favorite, but the odds did not seem to concern Lambeau. He felt it gave the Packers an added incentive. The kickoff was hours away, but the time seemed to be moving slowly.

Today, visiting teams go by bus to the stadium, but we left on the same subway Paul and I took to meet the Bears several years before. It was early Sunday, and many seats were occupied, but Paul stood over me and held a handle. I concentrated on his manner and thought he looked angry. I only saw him angry once before. Ironically, it was against the Giants in a game the year before when a player swung at him during a pass play.

It was before players wore facemasks and fists to the face were a way to intimidate an opponent, but the referee missed the infraction. Paul was enraged, but restrained by his teammates. The next several plays he crashed through the line with a spiteful force, knocking down the player who swung at him. He brought down the Giants back, "Tuffy" Lehman, with hard tackles just as he released a forward pass. They were not sacks, but his rush disrupted the play and forced the ball from reaching the intended receiver, as it fell to the ground incomplete. Paul had the same look now that he had over that incident.

I thought it was a good omen.

There were almost 50,000 spectators at the Polo Grounds that was filled with excitement, waiting for the game to start. It was mostly sunny day, but with some passing clouds. I watched Paul during pregame drills. Demie said his movement looked good, but I thought he had a slight hitch in his stride. There was no need for me to be concerned, not on this day. He dominated the line play and his injured knee never faltered. He stopped many plays on defense and was also a standout on offense, making blocks on the linebackers that enabled Green Bay to make important gains.

"Atta way to go, Paul," I heard a fan shout.

He was outstanding, and the Packers were in control of the game leading 14-0 at halftime. The Giants did not score until the first play of the fourth period, but Green Bay was now in control of the clock and the game..with a strong running plays. It would mean a win of the game and the championship for the Packers, 14-7.

Later, I heard a radio replay of the Packers' first touchdown. It was in the second quarter and Green Bay was on the one yard line. The Giants had stopped three thrusts into the line by Green Bay, but instead of kicking a field goal, Lambeau opted to go for a touchdown. It was a kind of "iffy" call, but I was in favorite of it. Both lines were bunched tight on the play. The Giants had a seven man line, plus four line backers to stop the

Packers. The play was not deceptive, only brute force. Paul blocked the Giant tackle with a move that pushed him back to create enough room for Ted Frsich to score a touchdown.

"It was the key block by Paul Berezney, the Rock of Granite from Fordham that enabled Frisch to cross the goal line, a radio announcer said in a recap of the Packers first touchdown. Paul played the kind of game he always wanted to have in New York. He was the best lineman on either side, as the reporter at the hotel said he had to be for Green Bay to win. On defense, he stopped every play that came at him, as well as several others that went in the opposite direction.

With the score 14-7 and Green Bay in possession of the ball for the remaining two minutes of the game, Lambeau sent a backup in for Paul. The crowd rose to cheer him in recognition of his outstanding game. He played 58 minutes. The next day, The New York Times sports columnist, Arthur Daley, paid him the ultimate tribute in his "Sports of The Times" column.

> *"The man who did the most operating in the Green Bay Packer line was Dr. Paul Berezney, the violent medico. Berezney graduated from Fordham and used his Green Bay salary to put himself through medical school. He is an outstanding example of the value of professional football to an enterprising young man"*

Arthur Daley's column was an accurate appraisal, but I realized Paul's football playing days were over. He had gotten all the game could give him, including a medical degree. Millions of dollars were not at stake for him to continue to play football.

It was a special ending to his football career.

The epilogue to the game came seventeen years later in 1961, when the Giants and Packers again faced each other for the NFL title. Neither team had vied for the crown since their 1944 meeting. Before he joined the Packers, Lombardi had a successful career as the offense coach of the New York Giants.

Newsweek magazine ran a report before the 1961 game that included predictions from Paul, "as the outstanding lineman," and Ward Cuff, "who scored the lone New York Giants touchdown." Cuff based his choice on the Giants to win "based on the strength of their team, led by Chuck Connerly at quarterback and Frank Gifford at halfback"

Paul's prediction for Green Bay to win was a brief statement."Vince Lombardi is the best coach in football," he said. Later, Lombardi called Paul to thank him for his exaggerated praise.

At first, Paul went into general practice as a doctor before he extended his medical career as a thoracic surgeon

The picture is of the Green Bay Packers' locker room at the Polo Grounds, NY, cheering their victory over the Giants in the 1944 NFL Championship game. Their coach, Early "Curly" Lambeau is being hoisted by several players. Paul is to the right in a jersey with a "47," next to "58," except Paul's number "4" is partially blocked out. The picture appears with the permission of the New York Daily News.

surgeon. I went to see him when he was in Tennessee to earn his Board Certification as a surgeon. He was an outstanding science student, but it was difficult to be admitted to medical school, despite his academic record. It took recommendations from several people, especially from Fordham. His prowess in football did not count, but his work in chemistry lab did. Ironically, when he graduated from Fordham he almost accepted a job in business, but John would not let him give up medicine as a doctor.

After a few days of my visit, I was surprised when Paul urged me to consider switching my college major to pre-med and go to medical school for us to ultimately be together as doctors, but I stayed with journalism.

At the hospital, besides the lead surgeon Paul was the senior surgical intern as part of the operating team. It was a strong staff, including two other interns and three nurses, plus an anaesthesiologist. One surgery was on a patient with a severe stomach ulcer. Paul and the lead doctor had already reviewed the best method for the surgery.

It was an astounding experience. On the morning of the procedure, we were up at 5:AM. I now knew why Paul had gone to bed early. I wish I had done the same. A stool was set up for me to stand on behind him during the surgery, which gave me a close up of the surgery. I had to scrub and wear a mask to be in the operating room that added to the drama. Bright lights glared down on us, but the air conditioning was kept at a cold temperature. I needed it to calm my tension.

I had never seen Paul so confident. He was more precise than in any football game. During the procedure, I worried about the patient, but Paul assured me he would recover completely. His report was more than uplifting. All I could think about was he was a surgeon and I saw him perform a critical operation.

Seeing him operate, I thought he was doing what he was born to do. Paul joked that he and Knute Rockne had chemistry and football in common. He taught chemistry before he became a coach. I'm sure Paul could have done the same, but he fulfilled his dream and became a doctor.

Too old for active duty during the Vietnam War, his greatest service may have been as a volunteer doctor in that war torn land. He was a member of an American Medical Association program that sent a team of doctors to Vietnam to provide aid to injured citizens, especially children, as well as to serve as a surgical consultant to an American military hospital. He seldom spoke about it, but he was proud of his medical service in Vietnam.

23
The Fighting Irish

With the help of my high school football coach, I got an after school job as a "stringer," or freelance reporter on local sports for the Hudson Dispatch, a newspaper published in Union City. I left reports at a Square newsstand, except an update on a basketball high school tournament was not picked up. I was called to the paper to complete the assignment.

I caught a bus at the Square that left me off near the paper, but was surprised that Lud Shabazian, the Sports Editor, would join the meeting. He was a renowned sports journalist, but I was surprised when he asked me about my brothers.

"I didn't know you heard of them," I said.

"Everyone in Hudson County knows about them and their football achievements," he said, "and after the game you played against St. Peters they know about you, too. "Wow," I didn't know what to say. I just nodded my head and said thanks.

When we completed the redo on the report, Lud said, "good job," and asked me if I needed a lift. I was going to take a bus to the Square, but he said he was going my way and would give me a ride. I knew his reputation for one line quips was unmatched, and wondered if I would be set up on the drive. He came up with one that was creative and involved us both. It was based on the need to spell our surnames so often.

He said it was all because of the letter "Z."

I knew a quip was coming and played along.

"I never heard the letter Z being responsible

for spelling my name before."Neither have I," he said. I just made it up and we both laughed.

Everyone who knew Lud said conversations with him always included a lot of laughter, but he quickly changed the subject and asked me about a more pragmatic, question not a quip.

"How did Pete choose to go to Notre Dame?"

It was a quantum leap arranged with Frank Leahy arranged by Johnny Druze, a native of Newark and a Fordham teammate of Paul. He kept tabs on New Jersey's high school players. He was alerted to Pete by several other coaches and recommended him to Frank Leahy, who had a quick response.

"I want a Berezney at Notre Dame"

Picture is of Pete at Notre Dame beside a bust of the
Knute Rockne. The picture appears with the permission
of *The New York Times* before the Army game in 1945.

Since Frank Leahy was one of Paul's coaches at Fordham, Paul was pleased to learn of his comment about Pete. It did not take long for his approval to be completed and he was on his way to Notre Dame.

After sitting up all night on a long train ride to South Bend, Pete said he was tired and skipped the bus for a taxi to the campus. He knew he would be attending one of America's great universities and wanted to arrive in style. As soon as he saw the Golden Dome, he said it only took several minutes for him to be overwhelmed by the campus.

Notre Dame is located on an Indiana plain that was once farmland, but with academic standards that exceed its football achievements. The school gained football prominence in 1913, when it beat a strong Army team, 35-13. As every schoolboy in South Bend knows, Notre Dame won the game with the forward pass before it became a significant offensive play. Gus Dorais threw the pass to a small end named, Knute Rockne and the school's place in national football prominence was established.

Pete entered Notre Dame forty years later and joined an elite football team that included six All Americans. They included John Yonaker at end, Jim White at tackle, Pat Filley at guard and Herb Coleman at center, as well as Angelo Bertelli at quarterback and Creighton Miller at halfback. Later. Ziggy Zarobski, the other tackle, was also named an All American to make the total seven.

Frank Leahy coached teams were known for their line play. They were big, strong and tough. Pete said Leahy did not change his demands at Notre Dame. The team's dominant talent of its linemen was apparent during weekly scrimmages. He said they were tougher than some of their games.

Notre Dame won the National Championship in 1943 with the help of a host of prominent freshmen to the top players listed above, including Pete and two running backs, Bob Kelly and Elmer Angsman. Johnny Lujack was the backup quarterback, who replaced Angelo Bertelli when he was called to active duty in the Marine Corps. With Lujack's talent, the team did not miss a beat

At the end of the season, Angelo Bertelli was awarded the Heisman trophy, the first for a Notre Dame player, but it was only the start. Several years later, Johnny Lujack, Bertelli's replacement also won the Heisman Trophy.

The Irish had strong teams in 1944 and 1945, but Army was unbeatable with a famous tandem of Doc Blanchard and Glenn Davis. The combination formed Mr. Inside and Mr. Outside of college football that overwhelmed opponents. Many college recruits were drafted or volunteered into the Armed services. Notre Dame's games against Army and Navy were highlight sports events in 1943 through 1945. Navy usually trailed Army, but it was much stronger in 1945.

Lud Shabazian knew about Notre Dame and its record, but he asked me about a game played against

Navy in 1945 at the Municipal Stadium in Cleveland. The game ended in a controversial tie. I later saw the game film and felt Notre Dame had made the winning touchdown.

Notre Dame scored the first touchdown for an early 6-0 lead, but it was tied on a tipped pass that was caught by an unexpected Navy defender, who ran with it to a 6-6 tie. The game became a series of top defensive plays by both teams, especially one by Pete on a reverse in an open field, when he evaded a block and made a tackle that created a big Navy loss.

The Irish came close to winning the game twice in dramatic fashion. The first was a pass play to the halfback, Phil Colella, who caught the ball at Navy's goal line, but was quickly yanked down. It was a close call, but the official ruled no touchdown.

There were 50,000 fans at the game. Half were sure Colella scored, while the other half felt the official made the right call. With less than a minute to play, Notre Dame had the ball on the Navy goal line, when Boley Danciewicz, the Notre quarterback, made two plunges into the Navy line to score a touchdown. Both failed.

Pete is the fourth from the left in the second row from
the top in the picture. Angelo Bertelli, Notre Dame's first
Heisman trophy winner is the second player to Pete's right.

Boley" Danciewicz made two moves called "sneak plays" into the Navy line. Pete was emphatic he scored on his second try. On the play, Danciewicz took the ball from the center and angled to his right behind Pete's block.

He was under the pile, where there was a lot of pulling for the ball. He said Danciewicz was just over the goal line with the ball. It took a while for the officials to get the pile uncovered, but it was ruled no score and the game ended in a tie. Lud said from the film he saw he thought Collela had scored on pass play, but that Danciewicz had made the touchdown.

Several years later, I met Lud at Robinson's, a restaurant at the Square. I had finished a tour in the Air Force and asked him to write a recommendation for me for a job. He said with all the good work I had done for the Hudson Dispatch, he was happy to do it.

"Any more stories," Lud asked?

I told him about a game Pete played when he was with the Baltimore Colts against the Cleveland Browns at the same stadium as Notre Dame's tie game against Navy. I was in my freshman year at West Virginia and drove to the game with Hal "Doc" Daugherty, from his home in Weirton, W.Va.

Hal was a star halfback at Ohio State and a friend of the Browns' end, Dante Lavelli, who also played for the Buckeyes. After a military career, Hal passed up football to sign a bonus contract to play baseball for the Detroit

Tigers and was attending West Virginia to complete his degree.

Pete was drafted by the Detroit Lions, but a new professional football group, the American Football League was formed in major cities. Many players from the National Football League signed with teams in the new league. One franchise was in Los Angles with a team named the "Dons." Their offer to Pete was twice what the Lions wanted to pay him, including a three year contract. It was too good an opportunity to ignore and Pete signed to play in Los Angeles.

Lee Artoe, who would become Pete's good friend, left the Chicago Bears to join him at the Dons. After the season, they were traded as a tandem to the Baltimore Colts. Lee Artoe said the Dons did not know what they were doing and predicted that he and Pete would prove it.

Pete played both offense and defense, but Lee Artoe was a defensive specialist. The Cleveland Browns and the Colts were two of the top teams in the new league. Several teams would merge into the NFL, including the San Francisco, Forty-Niners and the Cleveland Browns. The Baltimore Colts and the Buffalo Bills.The Browns were the best team in the new league for several years, led by Otto Graham, a top quarterback from Northwestern and Marion Motley a fullback from Minnosota.

Pete with the Baltimore Colts in 1946, when it was a franchise in the American Football League with teams in New York, San Francisco, Chicago, Baltimore, Cleveland and Buffalo.

The backup quarterback for the Colts was Y. A. Title, who later stared for the Giants. In the fourth quarter of the Colts trailed the Browns by two touchdowns. A punt put the ball on the Colts 20 yard line, but after a short gain the play of the game followed. The Colts had a strong passing game. Deep in their own end of the field, Charlie O'Rourke caught the Browns off guard. He faked a running play that froze the Brows linebacker. With Pete leading the way, he threw a short swing pass to Billy Hillenbrand.

A lot of the credit for what happened next went to Pete for the block he made on the Browns defensive halfback. He had come up fast to stop the play, but Pete took him down with an open field block. The stadium crowd rose to acknowledge him, as Hillenbrand went racing by for a touchdown.

"How'd you like that play," Pete called to me, as he sped past the bench

"Great, get another one," the coach shouted in return. He thought the comment was meant for him.

Lud laughed out loud.

Pete's football prowess was best expressed years later at a Notre Dame "Leahy's Lads" dinner of Frank Leahy coached teams. The group raised money to provide scholarships for qualified, needy students. The author of the book, "Leahy's Lads," Jack Connor, initiated the program with help of Gerry Groom, an All American center for the Irish.

I was with Pete and Elmer Angsman at one of the gatherings to honor rank Leahy. Elmer was an outstanding running back and Pete's teammate. He became a key player for the Chicago Cardinals in the National Football League. We were viewing the names of all the sports recipients of Monogram winners throughout Notre Dame's long history. They are listed on a panel circling a banquet room. The names are grouped within the decades that they attended Notre Dame, including the famous and the not so well known.

To cite only a few of the football players, they nclude Angelo Bertelli, Paul Hornung, Tim Brown, Joe Montana, George Gipp, Leon Hart, Johnny Lujack, George Connor, Johnny Lattner, Frank Tripuka, Emil Sitco, Jerome Bettis and on and on with the names of the players and Pete Berezney.

"There you are, Pete. You're in good company," Elmer said.

"You too," Pete replied.

That night, Elmer was the host at a special dinner to recognize players of the1945 Irish team.

"We've got our tackle with us tonight," Elmer said, "big Pete Berezney."

I thought it was a special recognition. Lud would have understood Elmer's compliment. He described the way he played the game.

It was not about dancing.

24

John's Car

The most disturbing fact about the Depression was it seemed we were never going to get out of it. The average worker earned little money, and Mike was surprised when John said he was going to buy a car. He had been driving since he was fifteen years old, which was not unusual in the 1930's.

He became a car buff.

Mike said he spent more time fixing cars than he did driving them. The car he bought was not new. It was a used vehicle, but like his other cars they had several problems. Mike only hoped it would run better than a "clunker" and was not a "heap."

The distinction is important.

A used car labeled a heap was in far worse condition than a clunker. There were a lot of them on the road, but a heap was an inferior car that was beyond repair. When a car was not performing, onlookers shouted a derisive comment at the driver.

"Get that heap off the road."

It was a criticism often heard in the 1930's. A car might be called a lemon, but no one wanted to be stuck driving a car labeled a sour fruit. During the Depression, most buyers could not raise the money to buy a new car, but many used cars were available, except some were clunkers.

John's latest purchase was a used sedan, which was an important factor. His other cars had been two seat roadsters that were great for a bachelor, but not for a family that wanted to see the world.

The arrangement is kind of odd, but here's the plan. The car was John's vehicle, but he would take us on Sunday drives through the Jersey countryside. For some wonderful reason, it was the way he wanted it, despite partying on a Saturday night.

There was a lot of excitement when he brought the car home, but the event turned into a disappointment. To everyone's dismay, John was not driving around the corner as everyone expected. He sat behind the wheel steering the car, but a horse was pulling it.

"Oh no," Mike said, "It's a heap."

My father hoped the car would run better than John's other cars, but the sight of it being pulled by a horse was both humorous and discouraging. The car had been in an accident and had a damaged bumper and right front fender. In addition, the right front door was damaged and the engine could not move without the horse pulling it.

My brother John, the family's leader and car buff.

"You got a piece of junk," Mike said.

"It's not, junk" John insisted.

"Let's see what you can do with it," Mike said.

After seeing the car being pulled by a horse, the neighbors agreed with Mike. What else could they think? They felt it would be hard for any repairs to correct the car's problems, so they did not linger.

The car was a recent model Buick with low mileage that had been in an accident. It was scheduled to be turned into scrap, but John saw its potential. He was confident the car could be fixed to run efficiently and was ready to go to work on it.

My father hoped he was right, but he was not sure. Since he did not drive, he couldn't offer an opinion. He rode to work with a worker, who had a car. In the family, we walked wherever we wanted to go or took a bus, which was one of the benefits of living in the city. We never seemed to miss having a car, but we would soon enjoy our Sunday drives.

John understood everyone's reactions, but he was certain the repairs would change their opinions. The first priority was to replace the damaged fender. He got one at a junk yard that was almost new and only needed to be repainted. When the door was refinished, it looked brand new. The work was done at a friend's yard, but John had to use the same horse and wagon from Keegan's stable to haul it to Bright Street,

"I can't believe it," Mike said. "Once more around the corner with the horse and we'll have to move to a new part of town."

John knew Mike's comments were said in jest, despite their implication. He repeated that the car was worth fixing or he would not have bought it. All that remained was to convince Mike he had made a good buy. The car was kept nearby on the Bright Street. It did not take long to see the progress.

After the fender was attached and the door was replaced, putting on a new bumper came next. Putting it on was harder than removing the damaged one, but my father's experience replacing damaged or worn steel plates with new ones to oil storage tanks helped. To be sure the bumper was secure, he double bolted it to the frame almost as good as it was attached by an assembly line. He had to go under the car to do it, which was difficult, but he felt proud.

"Great job, Pop," John said.

When they saw the repairs on the car the local residents on Bright Street were impressed, including Mike. With the body work complete, the jokes stopped and the compliments started, but when the car was moved alongside Keegan's stable to work on the engine, the comic references to the horse were recalled. The car's engine still did not run, but friends of John who were experts at fixing an automobile engine came to help. Later, he was adept at doing it.

Repairing the engine proved to be easier removing it from the car, but it had to be done piecemeal with parts strewn on oil stained blankets that were laid on the sidewalk. At night, with Jim Keegan's approval, the parts were wrapped in blankets and stored in the stable. Finally, after most of the engine was reassembled, it was ready to be put back in the car, but it had to be moved into the stable to do it.

With Mike's help, John installed a hoist and beams with chains to lift the engine into the car. It took time, but it was easy using the hoist. The required connections were made before the car was pushed out of the stable. After a check of the engine, it ran perfectly. John performed the final chore. He took the car on a test drive before John began our motoring excursion. On the day of our first drive, John polished the car, as my father and Pete were quick to exaggerate their compliments. We then joined what was America's favourite pastime, a Sunday drive to the rural countryside of lakes, small towns and farm views.

My mother prepared a special picnic. We went to Lake Hopatcong, a large lake in the northern part of the state that is a beautiful rural area. The front seat next to John was reserved for my father, while Pete and I sat in the back next to the windows with my mother in the middle. Mike was not with us or Paul, who was at college.

John gave my father a cigar before we left on our drive. What a sight it was to see a father and his eldest son, casually smoking cigars, as different as any two men could be, but united by the strongest bond nature ever created.

We went on many Sunday drives, but they were more than sightseeing excursions. John and my father discussed a myriad number of subjects, including: My parent's journey to America and my father's job at a coal mine. They discussed his work at the Sugarhouse and the oil refiner. The economy was at the top of the list to be reviewed.

It was educational, but hard to absorb it all. Paul's football games received special attention, as well as my father dancing the polka even though there was no connection between them. There were also comments on the road conditions that we encountered. The weather and the time it would take to get home was a prominent subjects. They were important to my mother. She did not like driving in the dark.

25

Mike – Hero and Renegade

It's easy to categorize my brothers.

John was the family leader with inner strength. Paul was the most intelligent family member, who became a professional football player and a surgeon. Pete was the standard bearer of patience, as well as an outstanding football player.

I was the impetuous one, but Mike could have been Mark Twain's choice to be Huckleberry Finn, wending his way down the Mississippi on a raft with a carefree spirit. He would have fit the role based on the many adventures he faced learning about life the hard way.

Mark Twain would have liked that about him. He was 5 feet 9 inches tall with a lean, muscular body that accented his narrow waist. When he was young he weighed 158 pounds. He had a small hair curl he pushed to one side that gave him a rakish look, but he also had a gentle personality that went with his likeable manner that went with his boyish enthusiasm.

Mostly, he had a sense of humor and laughed at difficult situations, but it was never easy. to do when he thought of them as minor problems, but his best feature was a smile that was pure Hollywood.

During the Depression, Mike left home trying to find a job. He traveled the country riding railroad boxcars from town to town and met many other jobless men like him trying to cope with economic problems. The Depression tested their confidence, but if Mike was unhappy, no one knew it. He never liked talking openly about the economy. Everyone said he had a strong core of independence, but he needed a job as much as anyone to feel useful. It was a deep personal feeling that threatened him.

As a sideline, he became a troubadour, who liked to entertain an audience singing old songs, but failed at doing a soft shoe dance. In the family, he was the vocalist, but John was the dancer. Watching them perform proved the designations were accurate, but Mike never gave up doing a dance in his routine. He remained as committed to singing and dancing, as he was about everything he did.

He had a patient manner that hid the serious side of his personality. He was not devious, but he knew how to turn on the charm. He lacked a college education, but epitomized what being street smart was all about. He was a bright, intense thinker. When he was older, he liked to discuss politics, the stock market, sports, religion and the meaning of life.

He had a viewpoint about all of them, but was willing to listen patiently to the views of others on any subject. He was a happy go lucky adventurer with an iron will to go with a pleasant smile. Above all, he was the most fearless person I have ever known.

The Depression soon brought distress to many Americans. After several discouraging attempts to find work, Mike joined an army of young men who trudged across the country, stopping whenever they heard there might be work to do. It was an elusive pursuit during an economic collapse, when it was impossible to find a job. Mike was "on the Road" away from home for over a year searching for a job.

As it was with so many others young men wandering the country to look for work, his sojourn was concentrated on going to California, but he had to make a dozen side stops to do it. He picked corn in Iowa, cut trees at a lumber camp in Colorado and worked at a copper mine in Arizona, but none were permanent jobs.

He lived with a farm family in Missouri doing odd tasks. Without knowing it, the farmer's daughter had an attraction for him, but he was not ready for a serious relationship, but she did. He thought it was innocent dalliance, but he left the farm to resume his travels.

"It was a narrow escape," he joked.

Being away from home for so long worried my mother. She often cried when Mike sent a letter from some far off part of the country. The distance was as hard for her to accept as his separation. It left her despondent, wondering when he would return home, or if he ever would. John kept hopes alive, saying Mike could handle his problems, but we shared my *mother's concernes.*

Nothing epitomized the severity of the time lost as much as the travails of unemployed young men who rode freight trains from one town to another, where they hoped they might be lucky and find work. Life without a job had no meaning, as Mike did.

Their travels brought no rewards, only a hardship they were barely able to overcome. Their youth had been stolen from them by an economy that could not fulfill their dreams. Trapped by the era's economic struggle, it made the 1930's a desperate decade. What the young men wanted to know was why they were caught in what they called "this God awful time."

Their wanderings were not an escape, but an attempt to find some purpose to their lives that only a job could give them, except there were no jobs at home or in towns where they stopped to search for work. It was an unparalleled period of hardship. Even Mike's description of his experience could not define the grim facts of what it was like to be a youthful job seeker, crisscrossing the country during a difficult economic time with 25 percent unemployment.

One day he returned as broke as he was when he left home without a job or money. It was upsetting to hear him relate stories of men making a reckless\ attempts to board a boxcar of a moving train. The movies have depicted men jumping on a boxcar as easy, but Mike saw many of the badly injured. I felt a deep regret over what he endured, but he spoke of his experiences as ordinary events.

He hid his distress when a story turned sombre, he would sing a song about the road to demonstrate his feelings. It was not a melodic, and the lyrics had a sense of sadness about the forced hardships of wandering.

The following condensed stanza is an expression of the basic problem the youth on the road met:

I knocked on the door to ask for some bread,
The lady said bum, you've been here before.
Why don't you work, like other folks do?
How can I work when there's no job to do?

The song was an anthem of road wanderers the country called "hobos," a defamatory designation. It was a harsh reminder of the pain the Great Depression had inflicted on the nation. Mike learned the meaning of the verse first hand.

After he returned from his extended sojourn, his decision to leave had not changed. His problems had remained unchanged. The economy was depressed and jobs were scarce. Some people were poor and starving. He was as penniless as he was when he left home, but he had a renewed conviction not to give up. He had a trove of stories about his travels, but his friends were mostly interested in hearing about Hollywood.

The movie capital was a magical place in the1930's, but Mike couldn't tell them what they wanted to hear.

He would have liked to have made it to "tinsel town," but he had a substitute to tell his friends. It was an expanse of beach not far from the movie capital that was nestled on the blue Pacific with rolling hills nearby. Mike worked at a grove picking oranges near the beach and spoke of it long before anyone on Bright Street ever heard of a place called Malibu that was destined to become a symbol of the good life in America.

He sounded as if he was describing some far off corner of the world, not the experience of a wandering victim caught in economic hardship. His description of his travels made everyone envious, but it brought him back to reality when they asked him how it felt to ride in rail boxcars. He would only say it was not comfortable, and they knew he did not want to talk about it.

My mother was not interested in stories about his travels. She was only glad he was safely home, but his life soon took an unexpected turn. He was at a gym where he was challenged to a fight in a boxing ring. To everyone's surprise he defeated his opponent, who was a professional fighter.

Winning the fight was the start of a budding career for him as a prize fighter. He entered several amateur events and won them all, many by knockouts. He was encouraged to become a professional fighter and trained hard. His quickness and attacking style made him a local favourite. He was soon popular in the city as a prize fighter.

After several consecutive victories, it seemed as if he was following a movie script, except it didn't last. Mike wanted to make boxing a career, but John said the promoter who signed him was only interested in making "a quick buck" from his popularity. He pushed Mike too fast to a fight above his class against a top professional fighter. Near the end of the final round, he took several hard blows to the head and sustained a severe concussion, which put boxing as an end tohis career.

It was a serious disappointment.

He was left with the same problems out of being out of work and nearly broke. Like so many men who struggled throughout the Depression, he was rescued by the economic build up to World War II. After his fighting career came to an abrupt end, he got a job as a welder at the shipyard where John worked. He was as proficient as a welder as he was a fighter riding boxcars. At special times, they were all important skills for him to know.

26
Summer Heat

It seemed we were always suffering from the weather with hot days in the summer and freezing cold in the winter. It was easier when we moved to rooms with warm radiators, but there were few ways to find relief from the summer's heat.

Air conditioning was still in the future, except several movie theatres had it, but not molty homes. At times, some business offices were forced to close early because of the heat, especially in old office buildings with windows that could not be opened. A cooling fan helped, but few on Bright Street had one, except for Mr. Rosen in his candy store.

A hot summer made it uncomfortable even in rural areas, but it was worse in the city when the temperature reached 90 degrees and the asphalt streets radiated the heat. It sizzled at bedtime when the heat hung like a warning sign of what was ahead for the night.

To get a night's sleep at 71 Bright Street, my father brought chairs from our dining room to set up as a bed at a front room window. He laid blankets on the chairs as a mattress and put a pillow over the window sill to rest his head, waiting for cool night air. Some people spent the whole night on their fire escape in hot weather. I wished I could do the same.

It was pleasant in June, but July and August were hot and humid, as rain storms came up from the South. The hot weather was hard to tolerate, except at the Jersey Shore, where an ocean breeze cooled the beach. We had enough of the heat and longed for a break in the weather, but cool nights didn't arrive until after mid-September. We were grateful for a break, but during the summer we heard the same complaint.

"Gosh, it's hot."

The heat was the principal topic during summer evenings, when there was a gathering on their front stoops or the sidewalk. It was common scene in the city, where no script was used and the dialog was usually restricted to the weather. The women were allowed to discuss recipes and bargain items that were on sale. At times, a few men joined the group to add their comments on baseball, but no one mentioned the economy. That subject was taboo and would have driven the temperature even higher.

"I hate it when it's this hot," someone said at the start of the session on summer.

"I'll never be able to get any sleep tonight," was a consistent negative appraisal.

"A newspaper said it was so hot in Chicago the eggs were cooked on the pavement."

"Can you believe that," someone asked?

"They could fry a dozen eggs on this street," a woman said to imply it was hotter than Chicago.

"I love the Shore. It always seems to be cool, but especially at night," a neighbor chipped with enthusiasm.

"The shore is the best way to beat the heat," another woman stated.

"Who has a car to drive to the beach," someone asked, without getting a response.

"Yesterday, it was hot at the beach," a new member of the group remarked.

"How can that happen," someone asked?

"I can't believe it" was another reply.

"You can never be sure at the beach. That's why I like a lake in the country" was a quick response. "You're right, it can be hot when the breeze comes off the land and not from the ocean," a male expert on the shore said.

"I still say the beach is the best place to find a cool breeze," another shore advocate insisted.

"I wish there was a breeze now. I would put it in a bottle to open when I went to bed to be refreshed by the cool air," an exasperated neighbor added.

Everyone laughed, but that ended the outdoor theater as the players left to retire for the night. Everyone waited for Fall season when the heat gave way to cool nights. If it was too hot, another late male group would gather.

Their wives insisted it was only an excuse for them to drink beer.

On such nights, my father was glad he had his bed of chairs. Some mornings after he left to go to work, I would stretch out on his makeshift bed and lay my head on the pillow over the window sill, as he did at night. I thought it was like sleeping outside and more comfortable than I imagined.

The outdoor meetings were one way for adults to escape the heat, but teenage boys chose another outlet. They went swimming at a waterfront inlet we called the Gap. There were two public pools in the city, but they were far from Bright Street. The proximity of the Gap added to its appeal, which made it our first choice to go for a swim. It was a popular escape, not as good as the beach, but the best we had. Pete learned how to swim at the Gap, and Paul took me on his back to get a ride on the Hudson River.

Sometimes, there were warnings about water pollution at the Gap, but they were usually ignored. No one ever became ill from swimming there, except sometimes on a cloudy day we skipped a swim and went to see a popular movie.

Another option my friends and I relied on for a respite from the heat was the fan in Mr. Rosen's candy store. We went into the store with the pretense to buy candy, but took turns in front of the fan.

We thought buying candy was a clever tactic to have time at the fan, except Mr. Rosen knew why we were there and often looked the other way from the fan. We called it a lucky day when he was occupied with customers, and we were able to spend more time being cooled.

One day, I was in the store when a woman came in to buy "loosies," or single cigarettes that sold for a penny each. Most brands cost ten cents a pack with twenty cigarettes. An additional ten cents could be made selling single cigarettes, but Mr. Rosen would not sell her any cigarettes. Other vendors did, but not Mr. Rosen.

He said it was not ladylike for women to smoke. I felt the same way. It was important for men to stick together to keep our traditions alive. It was long before anyone knew of the medical problems smoking could cause, but Mr. Rosen remained adamant. I was pleased with his reaction, but it also gave me more time in front of the fan.

At times, when he was busy Mr. Rosen was annoyed with our antics and forced us out of the store. He used a broom with stiff bristles to sweep across our feet to chase us out of stoor Once, he burned my ankle with the broom, which made me angry. He apologized, but told me to leave. Years later, I saw him and we laughed over our trying to be cooled by the fan and his refusal to sell cigarettes to women. I never mentioned being swept by his broom.

Next to having a car, I thought a fan was the most important item to own. A fan would make it easier for my father to sleep at night. I know I would have liked it, but young boys had a another way to beat the heat. They used a spray from a hydrant that turned Bright Street into a water park. If I made a list of my summer pleasures, water sprays from a city hydrant would rank at the top of the list with the Gap.

The hydrant was in front of the school and on a hot day a neighbor would appear with a wrench to open it. We bunched close together to witness the event, as if was a ceremonial rite of summer. The wrench was not an ordinary tool. It had a long handle needed for the leverage to turn the square edged brass faucet at the top of the hydrant. We stood in respectful silence watching its slow turns, as we waited for the water to pour out of the hydrant as a prelude to a special day.

The Fire Department said an open hydrant could decrease water pressure that could be a problem, if a fire occurred. Opening the hydrant was only a minor violation, but the Police stepped in and wanted to know who had the wrench. It was an important tool on the street and a scheme was developed to keep it from being discovered.

The wrench was moved each day from one house to another. Only the prior custodian knew where it was, as well as the new guardian. Someone said it was like a chess game, and the wrench was the king we had to protect. I could never guess who had it. None of the other kids cared, as long as it appeared when it was needed on a hot day.

John said hiding the wrench was an innocent subterfuge, but some parents feared an unexpected fire. They understood the dangers of low water pressure. To resolve the problem the hydrant water spay was monitored by the Police and Fire Departments. Later, a more formal agreement was reached to alow the hydrant to open three times a week in the summer on a limited time schedule managed by the Police that everyone approved. Many parents said the restrictions were sufficient to maintain water pressure in the event of a fire and tested the water pressure.

Making a street shower was a big part of beating the heat on a hot day for young boys and girls, but it required a skill using either a board or your butt. except no one wanted to use the board. It was not a challenge. All it took was to insert the board into the hydrant and protrude at an angle for an average spray.

Anyone could do that, but it was no fun.

Like most of the boys, I preferred using my butt, but there was a knack to doing it. You had to press against the hydrant, keeping your legs spread for the balance needed to make a strong spray. The more pressure put against the water, the higher and farther a spray would go, except there was always a line waiting to take a turn at the hydrant.

It was considered a macho experience. The older boys made the best sprays, but I was able to make mine go farther than it did with the board. The true test was to reach the steps of the rooms across the street.

Now, that was fun.

A lot of girls talked about doing it, but they never tried. Some of the older boys encouraged them, saying it would be fun to see a girl with her butt in the hydrant, but the only one who did it was a girl named Gloria. She wanted to show the boys she could do anything they could do, especially a water spray.

At eleven years old, Gloria was three years older than me with big thighs. When it was her turn, she ambled to the hydrant like Babe Ruth stepping up to the plate to hit a homerun. You knew she was going to make a top spray and I always cheered her.

Some of the boys did, too, but most of them were envious, as Gloria moved to take her turn. No boys could match the showers she made, but did not like it when she bragged about it, except they would stop to watch her do it.

I thought she was a nice person and we became good friends, especially during the summer when showers from a water hydrant were an important event on Bright Street.

27

Horseradish and Pork Rinds

Pete and I liked the city, but we wished we lived in a house in the country. We envied people who went to the Jersey Shore for the summer or only a weekend, which would have suited us.

We thought having a house at the Shore was for people who had a lot of money. We wished my father owned a car, but we would have settled for a telephone and a radio. Mostly, we wanted all the material things we saw, but did not have. Some were simple items like a football and dress shoes.

Poverty can be an indiscriminate intruder.

It depends on a person's needs, but during the Depression the record of families mired in economic difficulties was overwhelming. One thing we did not experience was hunger, as so many others did. I guess we were part of the lucky poor, if it's not a misnomer to equate my family that way.

We ate what some people thought were odd meals, such as tripe, which is the lining of a cow's stomach. It was inexpensive and a poor man's staple, but chewing it made it taste better. The low cost may have been why we ate it so often. My mother put tripe in a soup, which is the way my father and I liked it. John Mike and Pete didn't care for it, but they ate tripe not to offend our mother.

I was disappointed my friends did not share my enthusiasm for tripe. One of them was the poorest in our neighborhood and I worried about him. His father was out of work and his family had little money, but he said he would never eat tripe, even if he was hungry. He added that his father felt the same way and called it soggy animal guts. I thought he was missing a real treat. John said he could not be poor or he would eat a lot of food like tripe.

Chicken was our main Sunday meal, but at times we had a large cooked ham. My mother liked preparing both with a lot of vegetables, especially beets, attesting to our heritage. Most inhabitants of Eastern Europeans, including Rusyns love red beets. Sometimes we ate smoked fish for dinner that we got at a new Jewish delicatessen, but not on Saturday. It was inexpensive and a great fill in meal. I thought smoked fish was tastier than tripe, but like Pete, John advised me not to say that to our mother.

What I liked most were our holiday dinners

that Rusyns refer to our Christmas Eve repast as the "Holy Super." My parents treated it with a special reverence. Christmas was like a scene from a Charles

Dickens' story, where dinner was more important than most gifts. My mother's dinner at Easter was a feast, but what stood out was the ham she roasted. I thought our Easter dinner was as good as good as Christmas with hard boiled eggs and fresh stalks of horseradish.

To help her pay for our holiday dinners, she saved left over change from her food shopping that she put in a jar in our cupboard, including nickels, dimes and quarters, but no pennies. I often peeked at the cup to see how much was in it. There were always several dollar bills that I thought was lot of money, but my father wondered if it would be enough.

Somehow, she seemed to save the right amount of money to prepare food at each holiday. John said she got the food at Mr. Grossman's grocery with an agreement to pay for it later. Life in the 1930's was based on vendors like Mr. Grossman, who helped customers survive financially, including weeks without a holiday.

When she finished her preparations for either holiday, the food filled the dining room table, but my brothers and I were not allowed a small sample until priests from our Orthodox Church came to bless it. We looked forward to the sacred tradition, but my mother prevented us from eating even a nibble of what she prepared.

She covered the food with a table cloth that was secured at each corner. It reduced our temptation, but added drama to the unveiling when the priests arrived. We knew it was a special visit and waited for their coming, knowing how tasty her meals were going to be over the next several days.

At Christmas, my father made sure our rooms took on a special aura. He decorated the entry to the door to the dining room with evergreens. Their aroma added to the festive feelings of the season, and my mother tied small red bows on the branches that added to the holiday display.

For Easter, he filled two large vases with pussy willows, a unique plant with long stems and furry white buds. He often reminded my mother to bring home as many stems she could from church, where they were distributed. I thought they were special and fit the occasion as the fir tree branches did at Christmas.

Ham was my mother's main dish at Easter, as well as the bread she baked called paska. We could never get enough of it, but I thought her best item was kielbasa. It's a revered sausage in Europe and the U.S. To make it, she added several spices to a mix of ground beef and pork then put the mixture into animal links of skin. After they were cooked, she tied the ends of each link into an oval that she hung over the stove until they turned a rich brown that made them taste sweeter than kielbasa.

Of course, she prepared hard boiled eggs that were the perfect appetizer. We peeled the shells and sliced the eggs then scraped fresh horseradish over their roots to add to the taste of the eggs. The horseradish produced a spicy flavour, but there was always a contest on who was ahead eating the slight burning sensation of horseradish.

My father did not participate in the event, friendly as it was, but encouraged my brothers to add horseradish, applauding the winner. I still include kielbasa on my eggs, but only as a part of my Easter dinners. I have learned to be careful not to eat too much of the spicy horseradish root.

Most of the eggs we had were dyed a deep red, which is the predominant Rusyn color of Easter eggs, but the ones I liked the most were dyed a deep purple and dark blue. She also made intricate designs on the eggs we called "pysanka," but are more commonly referred to as "pysanky." It's an art form that began in Eastern Europe many years ago that has been passed on to succeeding generations, who brought it to America, where it has grown in popularity.

To create her designs, my mother used a needle as a stylus and without a guide she scrolled geometric or floral patterns on the eggs using hot wax. She immersed the eggs into a dye to color them, except where the wax was applied that made the designs stand out. Her work was excellent, but she was casual about it. Actually, it did require a sense of artistry and a steady hand to create the designs. When she finished, my father wanted to display as many of the eggs as possible, especially for the priests to see when they came to bless the food. They were genuinely exuberant about her egg designs.

"Krasne, krasne," they said, meaning beautiful.

When my father talked with the priests for a long time, we were sure it meant a large donation, but my mother always put money in a separate envelope for them. She would also give the priests several dyed eggs as gifts, which seemed to please them, as my father beamed.

Our daily meals were never special, but we had several traditional dishes for dinner. One was stuffed cabbage that Mike liked, but my first choice was pig's feet, or "studenina." My mother cooked them in a consommé spiced with paprika that she chilled in the ice box. I skipped the gelatin, but I ate the pig's feet. I thought they were a special treat. Finally, there is "piroghi" that are medium sized dumplings in the Rusyn spelling that everyone liked.

Piroghi are similar to other dumplings in many societies. My mother made them filling a pocket of dough with either sauerkraut, turnips or cheese and sometimes chopped beef. She folded the dough into a triangle shape and twisted the edges to make a tight seal, as well as to give it an appealing look. She sautéed them with onions, but at times she baked them. Piroghi was my father's favourite meal, but pigs feet remained my choice. John said he was split between the two, but he liked ham at Easter.

Despite the variety of foods, chicken was our most popular Sunday dinner. My mother bought one at a live chicken market. I often went with her when she made her selection. She said they were fresher than packaged chickens and cheaper. Live chickens cost eight to ten cents a pound, plus four cents to pluck and clean a bird, which was not small change to my mother.

The chickens were in separate cages stacked four feet high. She called the attendant to retrieve the one she thought would be the best bird for dinner. To see him remove the flaying creature from the cage was like a comedy routine from a Marx Brothers' film. He wore heavy gloves to hold the bird, but it continued to frantically flap its wings, as if it knew what was in store for it. I was impressed at how he held onto the chicken, but I also respected my mother's selection.

"Is it young," she asked as she fingering it?

"Of course," the attendant implored.

He held it firmly as she examined it, but to be sure of her choice, she made him show her another chicken. He was discouraged by her request, but not my mother. She remained determined, but maintained her patience.

"Look at this one," the salesman pleaded.

"Okay," she said, after examining it carefully.

When my mother was satisfied, the attendant was relieved. He knew he had a tough customer and quickly left to take the fowl to be processed. It was done in an open area that made it easy to observe. As the attendant began his routine, he looked at me with a sinister smile, as if to say he enjoyed his work and longed for an audience.

First, he deftly slit the chicken's neck and put it upside down in a metal tube as it twisted and scratched draining its blood. Next, he placed it in a boiling bath to make it easy to pluck its feathers and remove its intestines. When he finished, the chicken had little resemblance to what it looked like in the cage, but was now ready for the oven.

I'm glad chickens are not sold in open markets today, but it was an efficient procedure to get a young bird. When he finished his work, he wrapped it in wax paper and put it in a brown paper bag. My mother left satisfied, and I forgot the gory process. A happy meal can be built on a tasty chicken dinner, but I'm not sure I would want to watch the final preparation again, if chickens were sold that way now.

There's another episode about a food I want to mention. At times, my mother fried foods using pork rinds. She cut away the fat and gave me the gristle remains. Most people doubted it had any flavor, but I liked it. I thought it was a tasty morsel that I chewed until it was a soft white mass and went back for more. Once we had a food day at school and I brought some gristle to my class for my friends to know how special it was to get such good food.

I was disappointed when only a few students tried them, but spit them out into a dish on the teacher's desk. Of course, by the time I reached the school with the pork rinds they were cold and not as tasty as when they first came out of the frying pan. That was an important detail. The teacher had wrinkled her nose and refused the gristle.

"They're for the children," she said. I thought she was making a big mistake but she said that pork rinds were not really food.

"Not really food. Of course, its food," I said.

I began to chew on one of the pork rinds to show her what a special treat it was. I rubbed my stomach to demonstrate what she was missing, but she ate some feta cheese from a Greek boy instead. I could not believe she preferred his cheese.

What was a Greek doing in my neighborhood?

I made up my mind never to like Greeks, but he offered me some of his cheese to eat. I only took it to be polite, except I was surprised I liked it. I offered him a pork rind and he chewed it the way I did, smiling with delight. I began to like him and feta cheese, as well as all Greeks.

His name was George, but when the teacher commented on his cheese, he said it was made from goat's milk. I knew that was a mistake. The children heard his remark and spit out the cheese the way they did my pork rinds. I guess no one liked the idea of feta cheese made from goat's milk. He began to cry. I knew exactly how he felt, but my teacher kept trying to soothe him.

"Now George, now George," she said.

I felt left out and wished she had eased my hurt feelings, as she did for George and his cheese. I wanted her to say, "Now Steve, now Steve," the way she did for George, but she ignored me and my pork rind. I'm sure she would have liked it.

The idea to bring food to school turned out bad, but I felt my teacher was unfair to give him all her attention. I began to pull on her arm to get her attention, but she pushed me aside and took me to see the principal, saying I caused a ruckus in the classroom. She gave me a note to take to my mother that asked her to come to the school to meet with her and the principal. I was concerned and told my mother about it, especially my teacher's refusal to eat a pork rind. My mother was angry, but not with me. She thought my teacher had been rude. She would tolerate a lot of criticism, but not to her cooking. When she came to the school, the principal did not ask the teacher why she never ate a pork rind, but my mother. The principal's comment was how good my brothers were at school.

It did not take long for the plan to bring pork rinds and feta cheese to school was forgotten, but George and I remained friends until he moved away. Bright Street brought us together and it turned out better than I imagined waiting for good things to happen.

28
Beam WalK

"I never accept a dare," I said.

"Why not"?

"A dare always gets you in trouble."

"C'mon, you're scared."

"I'm not scared. I just won't do it.'

That was how it started when my friend, Billy Crawford dared me to jump on a beam floating in the water near the Gap. We were where we should not have been, as my fourth grade teacher, Ms. Evans, would say. Billy was always trying to get someone to do something he would not do, but everyone seemed to accept his dares, as I was tempted to do. The beams were bunched together in an unruly pattern with little space between them not far from where we could see the beams. They were about a foot square and eight feet long. Their size gave me the confidence to think I could jump onto one of them, except there was always a chance of something going wrong. The sun was going down and it was turning chilly, which meant it would not be long before the water would be cold. Trying to leap onto a beam floating in the water began to worry me. How did I get stuck in such a situation?

I just wanted to prove I could do it.

After we moved, I went to Bright Street often because my old neighborhood was special to me. I met Billy and we decided to walk to the waterfront, which was not far. It was Saturday before Thanksgiving. I had a happy anticipation of the holiday that extended to my good feelings, but I was hungry and wanted a hot dog.

I decided to go to a diner next to the Palace that had a service window for takeout orders. As we approached it, the aroma of chilli sauce and onions filled the air. I thought there was nothing tastier than a Texas wiener hot dog. Its enticing scent was almost as delicious as its taste. It was a perfect snack for ten cents, but Billy didn't have any money. I had twenty cents, but I needed a dime for my bus fare home, so I had to think twice about the spending money on a hot dog.

What the heck? What else were friends for?

I bought the two hot dogs, one for myself and the other for Billy. He gobbled his hot dog as if it was a Thanksgiving turkey. I thought he could at least have said "thanks," which would have satisfied me. I walked home from Bright Street before and I could do it again, except seeing him consume the hot dog made me wish I had saved the dime. I knew I would regret not having the bus fare home at the end of the day. There was another way to get home, but I never tried it. I could hitch a ride on the back of a bus, as many of my friends urged me to do. A friend on Bright Street we called "Horse" was adept at it. He liked to brag about his technique. He waited at a corner for passengers to be discharged and to pick up new riders. Horse said the timing was important. It required a leap on the back of the bus as it started to move. The trick was to place both feet on the slanted rear trim and reach around the edge of the bus to grasp the metal bars at the rear window and hang onto to the bars.

It was risky. I would never try to hitch a ride on a moving bus, but I should have been just as wary to jump on a floating beam. After we finished our hot dogs, Billy and I walked to the Gap, where we spotted the beams. There were over a dozen floating into the water. They had probably fallen off a barge and drifted close to the shore. I thought it would be easy to jump onto one of them.

The trick was to maintain my balance.

What was I afraid of?

Falling in the water, that's what.

How bad could that be?

Bad enough, I thought.

I hated the private conversation I was having with myself. I was caught in a mental tug of war over a dare, but it was a serious challenge I could not ignore. I did not want Billy telling everyone on Bright Street I was afraid to accept his dare, except I could be making a big mistake.

"I'll do it, if you will," I said. "Well," Billy said, but it was not a confident "well," but a doubtful, drawn out "w-e-l-l."

"Whata you say," thinking I had him?

"Okay," he said, "but you first go first."

"Me? Why do I have to go first?"

"Because I dared you to do it," Billy said.

"I'd go first, if I saw you do it, I said. s "What's the difference," he asked?

"The rules say the instigator goes first."

"Instigator, what's that," Billy asked?

"The instigator makes the dare," I said

"I never heard that before."

"My brother Mike told me about it."

"Is he an expert on dares?"

"That's the way it is," I said.

"Not with me," Billy replied.

I was tired of his objections, but I was stumped. Why had we walked along the waterfront? We could have found something else to do, or spent some time on Bright Street. I should have walked away, but like it or not, I felt I would have to accept the challenge.

"Okay, I'll do it," I said.

Billy clapped his hands and looked elated, which bothered me. We moved to the edge of the water and I thought he was going to jump out to one of the beams with me.

Yeah, fat chance!

He smiled, as if to say he was glad not to be the one making the jump. I always said the problem advantage in a dare is too one sided. There is no risk to the person making the dare only to the one who accepts it. It should be a shared responsibility, but it doesn't work that way.

I looked at the beams in the water and wondered how I agreed to do something as dumb to jump on a floating beam. When I looked at them, one of the beams seemed to be only several feet away, close enough for me to make the leap. I felt all I had to do was to steady myself when I landed on the beam. That was my plan. It's important to have a plan when you accept a dare. Mine was to maintain my balance when I landed on a beam, but I knew it would not be easy. Meanwhile, Billy was sporting a sly smile. I thought he looked the same way when he ate the hot dog I bought for him and never said, "Thanks."

What was he smiling about?

His smile made me angry.

He looked as if he knew something I did not know. I wanted to change my mind and tell him the heck with his dare. I was not a daredevil. Why was the word devil linked with the word dare? I did not want to be associated with the devil. Not me. Not ever. If there was a devil around here, it had to be Billy. When I thought about it, I wondered if he was really a friend. I began to doubt it.

"What are you waiting for," Billy asked.

"I'm planning my jump."

"Okay, but don't take all day. It's late."

"I'm gauging the distance," I said.

"Well, hurry up."

I looked at the water as I moved back to make a running leap to the beam. I hate dares I thought, as I made my jump and landed on the middle of the beam. It only tilted slightly, which helped me balance myself.

"I did it," I yelled.

"Yahoo," Billy responded.

I was pleased with my leap onto the beam and stretched my arms out to steady myself, as if I was a trapeze artist, but a moment later, I realized something was wrong. The beam was floating away from the shore. I had not counted on that happening.

After my jump, I thought it would be easy to get back on land, but now I wondered how I would do it. The beam kept drifting farther out from the shore, propelled by the force of my landing on it. I felt it would drift out even more. I knelt down and tried to paddle back to shore, but I couldn't do it. The beam continued to slowly make its way to deep water.

Billy yelled, asking what I was going to do. I wish I knew. It was your idea that got me out here on a beam, I said to myself. I regretted accepting his challenge. How about I dare you to jump out and take my place, I thought. Mostly, I was sorry I bought him the hot dog.

"Give me my ten cents," I yelled.

"What? I guess he didn't hear me.

Maybe he was really worried about me.

Then I had an idea.

There were other beams floating nearby. I could step from one beam to another one until I was close to the land. It gave me a renewed confidence and I made my move, except I was too hasty. I stepped on a nearby beam, but my left foot was too close to the end of the beam. My weight tipped it into the water and me with it. I went down quickly unable to see a thing.

It was an eerie experience.

The water was worse than black and I felt desperate. It was so cold it made my legs numb. Worst of all, my lungs felt as if they were going to burst. I knew I had to get above the water to breathe, but how?

Without thinking, I pressed my feet into the mushy bottom and bent my knees to push myself up as hard as I could. I broke out of the water thrashing wildly not knowing what to do, but I reached a nearby beam. I grabbed onto it with one arm and used my other arm to paddle my way back to shore.

It took a long time, but with Billy shouting his encouragements, but I made it back to land. I was dripping wet with my cap still on my head and water running down my face, as if I needed a reminder of what happened. I was shivering from almost drowning in cold water. I could not believe I had made it back to shore, but glad to be on dry land.

I sat down on a pile of old boards, as Billy pulled the cap off my head. He helped me take off my jacket and wrung it out, then stretched it over the boards and put his jacket around my shoulders, which helped me. I was glad he was with me, but I hated him. I could not get over using my bus fare to buy him a hot dog. If I had not accepted his dare, falling off a beam into the water would never have happened. Now, I wondered how I was going to get home.

"Did you enjoy the hot dog," I asked him?

"What are you talking about," Billy asked me?

"Did you enjoy the hot dog?"

"Yeah, sure," he said. "The hot dog was great. Thanks, but now we have to get you warm."

He was right and he said thanks for the hot dog. That was all I wanted to hear. Maybe spending the dime to buy him a hotdog was not a bad idea, but I had another problem. It was after four o'clock and turning colder. I was soaked and wondered where I could go to get dry. Then I had an idea.

"Let's go to the Sugarhouse," I said.

"Sure. It's not far and be open," Billy said.

The symbolism of the Sugarhouse was apparent and a saving refuge for my father. He replaced black coal dust with pure white sugar. Now, I hoped it would be a haven for me. Mostly, I needed to get my clothes dried.

We started running, but it was hard for me to keep up in wet shoes. I shivered all the way. There was a small office at the end of a building, but no one was in it. We went in to get warm, and I felt better immediately. I was still dripping water, but my shoes were no longer squishing. I needed to stay inside long enough to get my clothes and shoes dried, but I was concerned over how long it would take to do it.

"Take your clothes off," Billy said.

"Are you nuts? I can't take my clothes off. What if someone comes?

"Nothing will happen," Billy said

"You're crazy," I insisted.

"No I'm not," he said, "and you can explain everything. Besides, no one will find us."

"Yes they will. People are always here."

It was Billy's fault I almost drowned and now he wants me to take off my clothes. He was good at making dares, but not at anything else. I couldn't hold back any longer and I let him know how I felt.

"I wish it was you standing here soaking wet almost drowning over a stupid dare," I said. "I'd tell you to take your clothes off and to see how you felt."

"What are you kids doing in here," a man said.

A worker at the plant had interrupted my tirade. He was an African American. It was a Saturday and the plant was on short shift. I was trespassing and afraid he would order us out of the office.

"Hey kid," he said. "You're all wet." I kept quiet, as Billy explained my episode with the beam.

"I'll be," he said. "That was not smart."

He told me to take off my clothes and shoes so he could dry them. I looked at Billy and he just smiled. I undressed and my saver gave me a coat to wear, while he took my clothes, shoes and socks into the plant to dry in a kiln.

His name was Henry Blue and he was not angry over my being in the office. He was friendly and soon returned with my dried belongings. I told him that my father had worked at the Sugarhouse, and he was interested to hear about him. I liked him, and when I left he gave me a quarter for my bus ride home, which was more than the dime I needed. I thought about buying a Texas wiener hot dog with chili and onions before I skipped and left to get a bus.

29

Twuddy

To tell the story of my first pet, I have to go back a long time. I was almost five years old when I spotted him in a park with my mother, as we were coming home from food shopping. Someone had abandoned him and he was mewing and looking as helpless as a kitten could when it first opened its eyes. I picked him up and he nuzzled on my shoulder into my neck. I was content to let him stay there forever.

"What have you got?"

"It's a kitten. Can I keep him?"

I made my plea in an urgent tone. My mother could not believe someone had abandoned a kitten. I felt sure she would let me bring him home, but I used the best child's promise to keep a newfound pet.

"I'll take good care of him," I said.

She hesitated, adding he would have to be trained and sleep in the basement when he was older, except if it was cold.

"I'm a good trainer," I said.

Somehow, I knew we were going to be together for a long time. I thought it would be special for the both of us. He continued mewing, but I stroked him softly to soothe him. When we got home, my mother fixed a cushion in the corner of the kitchen for him to sleep with a barrier to contain him. She then tore newspapers into small strips that she put in a box opened at one end. She kept putting him in and out of the box telling him to do his "business." That's what she meant by training him. I thought she meant doing tricks. After several days, he learned what the service box was for in our rooms.

"What are you going to call him?"

My mother's question surprised me. I had not given any thought to a name, but I knew I would have to think of one. After several days, I told her I was going to call him "Twuddy." The name had no special relevance and I could not explain how I thought of it. John said just tell everyone he liked it.

Twuddy was an attractive cat with a black body, two white front paws, a partial white chest and a jaw area outlined in white on both sides of his mouth. He had an eye stopping appearance and was friendly, which I thought made him special. After three months, my mother took him out of the kitchen to the basement. I went down every morning before going to school to feed him. After school, I took him out to the backyard to frolic in the fresh air. He was happy to be outdoors, but so was I.

He was playful, as most kittens, but smart, too. I had a small red ball I used to amuse him. He loved to play with it and stretch out his paws to get ready to leap on it when I rolled the ball pass him. He kept his head down with his back arched and his tail in the air, poised to capture a playful intruder.

Twuddy seemed to be playing a game with me instead of the other way. After our play time he needed no encouragement to be petted. At times, I took him to bed with me, when Pete would let me. He liked that more than playing outdoors.

We went everywhere together, but he stayed close to my side, as if he was a trained dog. I would speak to him in a soft tone. He would tilt his head to one side to listen with rapt attention. In the evening, after my father had dinner, we played in the kitchen, so everyone could watch him perform.

John said he was the star and called it the "Twuddy Show." When we were outside, my friends rushed to see him. He soon became the best known pet in the neighborhood, which made me feel important. He followed me everywhere. When I went to Mr. Rosen's store, he went with me. I would tell him to stay close and wait for me. People passed him on their way in and out of the store, but he was unperturbed. Mr. Rosen would lean out from behind the door to see if he was there.

"Look at that cat. He's waiting for this kid," he said to customers. "Did you ever see a cat like him? My mother had a unique theory about cats. She felt he belonged to the outdoors, as much as he did to a home. It was okay with me, as long as he returned after a reasonable time, which he always did. I was glad he was learning to live by his instincts. He would never wander far, but it was pleasing to see how much he liked being with me. When he grew older, he would be gone for several days, but he always returned to play with me.

I know it sounds odd to let him roam, but it seemed to strengthen our bond. Some people have a cat as a pet, but they can never let him roam for fear they would lose him. Twuddy always returned and never gave up purring his contentment to see me. I would talk to him softly and felt he liked being with me as I did with him. There was nothing different between us. The love of a pet can make you believe anything.

Once, an incident occurred that made him popular on Bright Street and convinced everyone he was not an ordinary cat. He caught a small bird and ran away with it in his mouth under a tenement stairway. A group of boys ran after him, shouting to let go of the bird, but he kept hold of his prey. I was playing nearby and called to help. I hurried to the scene and knelt down to get as close to him as I could. When he saw me, I knew he would do what I asked.

Without pleading, I told him to let the bird go.

Twuddy was a hunter, pleased with his catch, but he came out from under the stairway and released the bird. The stunned avian laid motionless, then quickly right itself and flew away. I picked him up to stroke as he purred his contentment. He put his face against mine to rub against my cheeks, as if it was a reward for his good deed. He looked up at me, as we walked home with his head turned to me. I kept talking to him, telling him how good he was. Everyone seemed stunned, but I felt sure he would let the bird go, if I asked him. After his released his they believed he was not an ordinary pet.

"I can't believe he let the bird go," someone said.

One evening, soon after, I went with Pete and several friends to a movie. Twuddy walked by my side, but friends laughed when I told him to wait for me, but when I came out several hours later I knew he had not gone far. I called out his name and he came running to me. Pete's friends did not believe he would wait for me, but I knew he would be nearby.

I told my mother what happened, but she doubted what I said, as Pete's friends did. I was disappointed she did not understand the bond that existed between us. She was with me when I found him, and I thought she knew how much Twuddy and I cared for each other. Our feelings were based on a commitment of mutual trust. People who have a pet know what I mean. He just followed my lead. The closeness we shared can never be fully explained. Was it a law of nature? Who knows? I'm not sure what it was, but it was there for Twuddy.

Call it animal love.

Ultimately, the decision was made for us to move from Bright Street to Chestnut Avenue, a long distance. It was necessary for the man, who drove my father to work to meet him. Twuddy had not been home for several days before our moving date. No one I asked had seen him. My mother joked he was busy seeing the world, but I didn't laugh. I regretted I had let him go on one of his junkets, so close to our move. I worried about him, but my mother insisted we couldn't wait any longer.

I was afraid I might never see him again, but she said I could go back to Bright Street with Pete to look for him, which made me feel better. I always left a window open for him to get into our basement, but there would be no open window he could use now. I was concerned over what might have happened to him and blamed myself.

What would I do without him?

A week later, Pete and I set out on our search mission. My mother said she thought it was hopeless. She felt we would not find him, which troubled me. We made our way to Newark Avenue, a busy four lane thoroughfare with traffic going by in both in different directions. As we started out, I thought we would keep to the right side of the street in the same direction as the traffic going to the East downtown, but for some reason Pete crossed over to the other side of the street. I followed his lead, but after we walked less than two blocks, Pete made a startling observation.

"Look, there he is across the street.'

I could not believe it. I thought he was teasing me, but when I looked up, I was gripped with a strong feeling of euphoria. Could it be?

"Yes! Yes!" I shouted.

It was Twuddy. He was moving with his head weaving back and forth, sniffing his way to me, only a short distance to our new rooms. I was thrilled.

"Twuddy," I called out.

Suddenly, I was afraid it was a mistake t0 call him, as speeding traffic raced passed us. What would I do if he was struck by a car as he was crossing the street, but he ignored the danger and bolted pass the traffic to jump into my arms, something cats never do. He let out all his love for me, mewing as he cuddled at the side of my neck the way he did as a kitten when I found him. All I could do was continue to mention his name and pet him.

It was a wonderful moment.

I love all animals, but Twuddy had my heart.

It was a long trek from Bright Street to our new rooms. Maybe a dog could have found me, but not a cat. How did he do it? It was a week after we moved. We left in John's car and used a friend's truck to carry our furniture. There was no scent for him to follow, but somehow he found me from an instinct instilled in him millenniums ago.

I know he would have traced the route to my door. It was an impossible task, but he did it. I wanted to believe he followed my longing for him. People say cats belong to a house, but not Twuddy. The home he knew did not matter without me. It was a long distance, but he was determined to find me, no matter how far he had to go.

We had seven more years together. At first they were good years, but later there were problems. He came and went as he did before, but there was no open window in the basement for him. He also did not like going up down the hall stairs, especially to the top floor, where we now lived. We played together a lot on Saturdays at a park. One morning, my mother let him out early, but when I came home from school he was not waiting for me, as he usually did.

He was in the backyard on his side. Twuddy would never walk with me again. He had died. I knew I had to bury him and thought of putting him in the park where I found him, but John said it would be better to do it in the back yard.

I knew he was right. I wrapped him in a pillow and put him in a round metal candy case my mother gave me. It was a red container with a floral pattern on the cover. I dug a hole in the yard two feet deep and lined it with stones. I put him in the ground and poured a concrete mix over him John had prepared.

When the concrete dried, I covered the area with bricks snugly in the ground in a square pattern, as a marker of where I buried him. I went to check it often, but over time I could not keep the bricks clear of the invading grass. I was left with only the memory of where I buried him.

Twuddy meant so much to me growing up, it would have been impossible not to include him in this story. He was an important member of my family.

30

A Cossack Dance

Jersey City was replete with Irish bars, including one at Newark and Chestnut Avenues, a short block from where we lived. It was a typical of most working men's bars with an aroma of draft beer. A shot of whisky was all it took to make it fade away, so the regular customers ignored it.

At the time, an important law was in effect at city bars. They did not admit women. It was like an invisible wall that male patrons supported, but did not apply to restaurant bars. They wanted a refuge at a bar with a shot or two of whiskey without female interruption. They brought their good feelings with them, but still spent a lot of time discussing women. What else? They talked a lot about sports. At times, it led to an argument. Politics was often a topic. Any subject was open for discussion as long as it wasn't personal and no one ordered a cocktail.

A cocktail was considered a lady's drink. The men wanted a straight whiskey in a shot glass with a half glass of beer as a chaser. The combination had a tough sounding name to match the potency of the drink. It was called a "boilermaker," a man's drink. Nothing was more popular at Irish bars in the city.

My father was not a regular, but he could drink with the best of them. At times, he wanted to do some male bonding and "socialize," as he referred to it, but the Irish bar was what he had in mind. He didn't like going out to drink, as he did when he was younger. It was a Saturday and getting late. My mother was concerned he might need help and sent me to get him "just in case." I was happy to do it and knew where to find him.

The bar had dim lights set in a high ceiling that kept the lighting subdued, but in the daytime and summer evenings, such as this one, sunlight came in from two large front windows to give it a cheerful look. It was after 5:00 PM, but I knew I would have no trouble being admitted, despite my age. I was on a rescue mission, which was an exception to the law for minors, but a routine had to be followed.

It included a peek inside a side door to call out the name of the person you wanted and the patience to wait for a response. It took time, especially during the so called social hours, but my father was well known and the bar tender came quickly.

"C'mon in" he said, "you'll enjoy this"

When I entered the bar, there was a commotion from a crowd that had gathered around one of his drinking buddies. He was standing on a chair making a wager about a dance he wanted my father to do. I was concerned when I heard his proposal.

"I bet Sugarhouse Pete can do a Cossack dance."

Oh no, I could not believe it. I was glad I got to the bar when I did. My father was not ready to do the dance, but bragged he could do it, as most East Europeons said they did it when they were young to impress young girls. They liked the dance, but not the country associated with it. My father was a forty year old had something to prove. I had heard him talk about it and knew it would take a strong argument to convince him not to try to do it. He would want to prove his agility, especially in a bar with friends.

That's how it was when he made up his mind. I was glad I got to the bar when I did. His friend, who promoted the bet was a short, squat Irishman, standing on a chair with his arms stretched out in front him. He had a fist full of green bills in his hand that made him looked like a giant pitchman. He was in control and had created an excitement in the bar with his bet, except in his haste he slipped coming down from the chair too quickly. He fell to the floor and let out a loud fart."Shit," he cried.

"You said it," the bartender shouted, and the bar exploded in laughter. The odds against my father felt a Cossack dance went up fast that created a rush to take up the bet. He was a selective drinker, who thought he could do anything after several drinks, and he already had several. I was concerned he might end up the way his friend did on the floor. Despite movie versions of young dancers doing a Cossack dance with high leg kicks, it was not easy, and I did not want to see my father ridiculed over something so trivial.

I had to get him home, but he pretended not to hear me when I asked him to leave. He was determined to demonstrate his skill, as he downed a swig of beer. He considered having a whiskey, but waved off the bartender, saying he was ready. My confidence rose with his good sense, but not my conviction.

He moved to the center of the bar area with a serious look. A circle of men engulfed him, but they left enough room for him to maneuver as he stood poised waiting to perform. There was no music, only a rhythmic clapping that seemed to encourage him to show off his talent.

It was an exciting scene.

I felt proud clapping with the crowd. He had talked about teenage boys in his homeland doing the dance and learned from them. With his arms crossed in front of him, he did a perfect rendition of the dance, and kicked out each leg amid rousing cheers.

When he made a high leg kick and shouted, "Hey," the crowd acknowledged him with a loud "hey" in return. He quickened his pace that electrified the patrons and a chorus of cheers grew louder. I was as excited as the crowd that surrounded him, but I couldn't believe his performance.

"Atta way to go Pop," I shouted.

How long did it last?

Was it two or three minutes?

It was not longer.

What he did was enough.

I was astounded to see him do the dance, calm as he was, especially after all my doubts. When he had finished, he rose from dancing in a nonchalant way. The men in the bar were impressed. I joined the crowd with a loud round of applause.

"Wow" was all I could say.

The only thing he did not do was to leap and touch the tip of his shoes, but what he did was more than enough to satisfy his drinking pal, who was busy collecting the bets. My father was pleased, shaking hands with the group that surrounded him. They patted him on the back, even the losers who bet against him. They knew they had seen a special show. He enjoyed the accolades, but refused a shot of whiskey and drank a swig of beer.

"C'mon Pop, let's go," I said.

As we turned to leave, his pal stuffed some bills into his shirt pocket. I led him out of the bar and the early night air refreshed him. We felt relieved and laughed without holding back our good feelings. It was getting dark, as we trudged slowly on our way to the corner to our rooms across the street. We faced another obstacle to climb four concrete steps to the entrance. I offered him my arm as support, but he said he was okay.

We climbed the concrete steps and entered the hall, where we faced a more difficult prospect of "Mt. Everest," as we called the top floor to our rooms. There were three long flights to climb. I usually took them two at a time, but I wouldn't be able to do it now with our usual confidence. Each flight was a slow ascent, but we made our way up the stairs. I thought of his dance when he moved so nimbly. Now, he had to steady himself, but he smiled and said don't worry he was okay. That reassured me. When we reached the top floor, my mother heard us and opened the door.

Is he all right," she asked.

"Yes," I said, "but you should have seen him."

I told her about the dance, but she only smiled with a weak compliment. I was disappointed she was not more enthusiastic, but getting him to bed was on her mind. He was willing and glad to have the help.

We lived in railroad rooms, a common layout in the city. The rooms were in a straight line from the kitchen to the front room with three bedrooms in between. No doors separated the bedrooms with ample space for a bed and an area to pass from one bedroom to the next. The last one opened to comparing the front room, where my mother and father slept.

To get to his bed was no trick just easier than climbing stairs, and he cooperated with my mother, holding his arm. She him easily, reaching his bed was the final challenge to a special night, but she had little trouble getting him settled. It only took several minutes and not long before he was asleep. I thought he had put on a great show and earned the rest. I guess my mother did, too.

The next morning was no ditterence. It was Sunday and he got up at 5:30 AM, as he did to go to work, but my mother said he was energetic. He ate a hearty breakfast that included eggs, toast and coffee. He finished his meal without saying a word about the previous night.

I could not believe he never bragged about his performance. I know I would, but she said he never mentioned it or the bet. I was disappointed that he did not tell her about the dance, but I guess doing it was enough of an accomplishment for him. It was his style. I knew he loved to do the polka, but now he could add a Cossack dance to his list.

31

Intercepted Pass

Jersey City once had a sports stadium named after President Roosevelt, where separate Triple-A minor league teams from the city with the same name with major league franchises that played both baseball and football. The Jersey City teams were called the Giants. I saw Jackie Robinson play his first professional baseball game there against the Giants with a Montreal team before he joined the Brooklyn Dodgers in the Major Leagues.

The Stadium had lights and several of the city's high school teams played Friday night football games there. At Dickinson, we played our home games on Saturday afternoons at the High School Field. There were no lights, except we played our traditional Thanksgiving Day game against St. Peter's at Roosevelt Stadium before a large crowd.

One Friday night, I went to see my friend Demie Manieri play an important game at the stadium. He was the quarterback for Lincoln High School, directing their offense and I wanted to get an insight into their strengths.

My friendship with Demie began in elementary school. He lived close to the school and often invited me to lunch at his house, so it did not take long for me to get to know his family, as he got to know mine. Once, when we were in high school, we "played hooky to" skip a day of school to see Frank Sinatra to sing a few songs we liked at the Paramount theater in New York. We were

Sinatra fans, and it was his first stage appearance in the city. A special day for us.

After his performance, we decided to see his show again and moved to seats closer to the stage. The seats were great, but we had to sit through a repeat showing of an ordinary film. When Sinatra came on again, some young females in the audience made it to the stage trying to get close to Sinatra. They put on a show of their own. A small group made it to the stage with a barrage of shrieks, but Sinatra remained calm and patient waiting for them to be escorted out. It was quite a scene that was reported in the press.

Demie and I were preparing for another kind of show, opposing each other in a football game. Lincoln was having an up and down season, similar to our games at Dickins we should have won. Football is a physical game, but it also has an element of strategy that can mean the difference in winning or losing. Lincoln was that kind of team. It could beat an opponent with a surprise play, not a tricky one, but an unexpected play made it exciting to watch.

One play was effective for Lincoln the moment I saw it. It was a pass in the red zone, which is inside the 20 yard line, relatively close to the goal line. I knew it was a good play. It started as a run, but ended as a short pass to Demie, who was left unopposed for an easy touchdown.

A pass in the red zone was seldom thrown in high school football in the 1940's, but every team playing Lincoln had to prepare for a run or a pass close to the goal line. It's easy to describe, but a fast moving play in a game put pressure on the defense and made it difficult to defend against Lincoln

I was the backup quarterback for Dickinson waiting for my chance to throw a pass for the winning touchdown. But two weeks before our game with Lincoln, I was surprised when my coach, Stan Shableski, who I admired, asked me to make a surprising switch from quarterback to center.

I coun't do that, I swore.

My coach said we needed to strengthen our defense. I had speed and was the best tackler on the team. Football players once played both offense and defense. The center on offense was a linebacker on defense, but I was not sure it was the right move for me. My coach said I would play the whole game and it would make the team a winner.

That was it for me. I made the change.

My first test was against Ferris High School, a strong city rival that was favored to win our game, but Johnny Payne, their top running back was hurt and did not play. We played a strong game without him that enabled us to gain an 18-0 upset win. I made several important defensive plays to prevent a first down to stop a surge by Ferris. I also rushed the passer on a play that caught him for a critical sack.

Ed Friel, the Jersey Observer's sports reporter, a city newspaper, added to my good feelings in his report on the game. He wrote:

"Steve Berezney switched from quarterback to center in Dickinson's big win over Ferris and what a game he played."

After the game, we were 2-0 in the county, including an earlier win over Snyder, another city rival. Our overall record would be four wins, if we won our games against Lincoln and St. Peter's. Two more wins would represent a strong comeback and place us in contention for the Hudson County title, except that Memorial High School in West New York was everyone's choice as the best team. First, we had to beat Lincoln and then St. Peter's, but I knew winning either game would not be easy.

I went to see Demie the night before our game, but he was surprised by my visit. I guess it was like fraternizing with the enemy, except we were soon in the kitchen eating cake, needling each other over our rivalry. His father came in and referred to us with a special metaphor he used. He called us "Engineers," who were always hurrying somewhere like a speeding train.

"Two engineers are going to play," he said.

"Who is going to win?"

"Lincoln," I answered.

"Dickinson," Demie said.

We laughed over our polite predictions, as we showed our respect for each other, but I knew it would be a tough game. I think Demie felt the same way. The next day before the game his brother wanted to take our picture on the field before the game, but when I asked my coach for permission he did not like the idea of posing with a player from the opposing team. I said we were close friends and had gone to elementary school together.

"Okay," he said, but take the picture at midfield." I thought I might have a problem later, except for what happened in the game. After the first half, we were leading, 19-7, so much for our predictions, but my coach was unhappy. Only a few plays enabled us to be ahead in what he called a sloppy game.

If our coach hated anything, it was inept play. He lectured us about it during halftime, especially how to handle an over shift Lincoln was using on defense. He diagramed it on a chalk board and emphasized a defense that would succeed especially against a running ppay. It took a while for an over shift to become common in football, but it was innovative for Lincoln.

I was surprised how relaxed I felt in our game especially during the first half. Demie and I were talking to each other, which was a scenario we had been through many times in our school yard. There were more than several players I knew one Lincoln used. I was chatting with most of them. One was Frank Orrico, who became a successful dentist in the city. Another was Frank Vitalle, an outstanding guard, who went on to become a standout lineman at Cornell. I also knew Joe Marshello, Lincoln's top forward passer, but he was hurt and did not play.

We were winning the game and having a good time. I was having fun, except I should have realized nothing would be settled early. After the kickoff to start the second half, I felt that Demie would lead Lincoln to a comeback and marched it down the field. There were no long plays. Twice it made a first down on a two yard gain, and once they made a first down when I was sure we would stop them.

The drive took almost the entire third quarter, all on running plays. Lincoln had reached our 15 yard line and was threatening to score. Only three yards kept it from a first down and a possible touchdown that would cut our lead to 19-14 and shift the momentum to Lincoln. It was a perfect set up for an unexpected play, and I knew Demie had one.

When Lincoln came out of the huddle, I kept my eye on the halfback. I wondered what play had been called, a run or a pass. Getting the first down seemed to be the most likely prospect. It would give Lincoln four downs to continue their drive, but I looked at Demie and thought it was more important to be ready for a pass and I moved a step to my right.

It was a critical decision.

As the play developed, everything seemed to move in slow motion. I glanced at the halfback and saw him take several steps to his right, then stopped and turned. I felt he was setting up to throw the pass to Demie, who had moved a few yards toward the sideline. I was ready and took a step to my right, away from the running play. It was a chance, but I knew I was right.

Throw it. Throw the ball, I said.

I saw the football spiral toward Demie and raced to make an interception. My coach said a single play can mean the difference between winning and losing. You have to make the play. I wondered what his reaction would have been if I dropped the ball, but I didn't drop it. I reached up and grasped it then raced down the field. I heard the cheers from the stands that spurred me on to make a touchdown.

When I crossed the goal line, I waited for the referee to see that I was in the end zone. I smiled when he raised his arms signaling a touchdown that made the score, 25-7 in our favor.

In the locker room after the game my coach singled me out to say great game. Pete's close friend, George Simonelli, who played with him in high school was at the game. He was a terrific player, who had returned from European duty with the Army Air Corps during World War II. His plane was shot down on a raid over Romania and he had to bail out. He was captured by the Germans and became a prisoner of War for eleven months. He was subjected to severe conditions, but rescued by a contingent of the American Army near the end of the war. George was a real hero. He was at the game and said I made an excellent play. I took it as a compliment from Frank Leahy.

A group of cheering fans carried me off the field. I saw my father and waved to him. He nodded, but stayed in the background. He had a slight smile and a pleased look, which was all I needed to know he had seen me play. His nod seemed to say "good job."

It was enough for me.

The play made my season. Beating Lincoln put us in position to contend for a share of the county championship, if we beat St. Peter's on Thanksgiving Day. There was a light rain falling and the game was postponed to Saturday. I was disappointed.

Mostly, I missed the tradition of playing on Thanksgiving Day. I wanted to celebrate with a holiday dinner. By noon the weather had cleared and the field was in good condition, except the game had been rescheduled.

What we knew about St Peter's was they would be well prepared by their coach Bill Cochran. He was a quiet, disciplined man, but I was confident we would win. My coach felt the same way. It had been a long season, but we worked hard to forge ahead from a bad start. Now, we wanted our efforts to culminate in a win. Our coach had a simple message.

"Play tough," he said.

The game was 0-0 until the last play of the first half when a halfback option pass was badly thrown into the arms of a St. Peter's defender. He was surprised, but raced down the sideline for a 6-0 lead. We mounted a strong third period, but it faltered and St. Peter's won the game. I was disappointed, but I made several important tackles. Two of them were inside our five yard line that stopped touchdowns.

Football has been a large part of my early life, following two brothers, who played the game at such a high level. I was trying to create a record of my own, but I never equaled what they accomplished. My brother Mike was at the St. Peter's game and made it to my locker room. He knew how I felt, and said I was a better player than my brothers. He was only trying to make me feel good and I loved him for it.

After the season, my most grateful news was to be named as Honorable Mention at center to Jersey Journal's All County team. I had only played three games at center, but I was appreciative of the paper's recognition.

32

The World of Tomorrow

The 1939-1940 World's Fair was the perfect climax to overcome the rages of the Great Depression. Only the one to commemorate the nation's Centennial in Philadelphia in 1876 may have surpassed it, but many historians doubt it.

News reports stated the Fair was a look into the future called: The World of Tomorrow. The motto pleased everyone, especially with the symbols created to represent the Fair. Their names were as dramatic as their futuristic designs. One was a three sided obelisk called the Trylon that rose 700 feet to a tapered point. The other was a perfect Perisphere with a 200 foot circumference.

Standing side by side in a startling white color at the Fair's entrance, they were an example of the melding of art and technology. If you drove past the Fair on Long Island, they were easily visible, as were their miniature replicas that became so popular they seemed to be on display everywhere.

A couple of city dudes, Pete and I in Jersey City.

The symbols seemed to become as prominent as the American Eagle. After the "hard times" of the Depression, the Fair seemed to represent the hopes the people had in the future. We had survived a serious recession and were ready to move ahead to a new and better[1] time of economic growth, despite a hovering threat of war. As a nation, we could not be denied.

It was our time.

The World's Fair was a testimonial to the nation's growing strength and one of the reasons for our new found enthusiasm. We put it on display for the world to see we were ready to rebuild our economy and our country.

Several Government programs to combat future economic setbacks became laws, including: A Federal Deposit Insurance Corporation that insured most Bank deposits. A new law to support elderly Americans called Social Security provided a retirement income for the elderly. A Union of workers and a Fair Labor Standards Act established the first hourly wage at $.25 cents an hour, a meagre amount. It was barely sufficient in 1941, but the rate was challenged by economists, but labelled the start of the Middle Class.

There should be little to care about a decade filled with so much hardship, but historical analysis often dotes on disaster. The Great Depression had enough negative experiences to satisfy any challenge, but a combative citizenry also had to rise up to win a threatening war that saved the nation and was recognized as "America's Greatest Generation."

Mike went to the Fair several times and spoke of it often to create a lot of excitement in our house. My father asked John to get tickets for us to the Fair. We went on a weekend in1940, close to its closing. I was excited and wanted to see it all in one day. Everyone said it could not be done, but I wanted to try.

When we arrived, I could hardly contain my enthusiasm. I didn't know what exhibit to see first. Mostly, I wanted to go on the Parachute Jump that was not a jump, but a swift drop in a parachute. My father said it was not for him. I needed an adult substitute to take the ride with me, but did not take long to find an anxious companion.

It was designed for adults, as much as it was for teenagers. Riders were lifted 250 feet up then dropped to the ground. It took over forty seconds to be hoisted to the top of the tower that provided a wide spectacular view of the Fair, but only ten seconds back to the ground. The first 50 feet was like a free fall with a bungee like thrill, but the swift descent felt like a threatening sensation, except it was what made it popular. When the chute opened, it became a pleasant release, as it floated to the ground. A big part of the ride was in anticipation of coming down so fast.

The best exhibit at the Fair was the General Motors display, called "Futurama" that presented a unique look into the future. We sat on a moving chair above a scale model of what America would be like in 1960, as a recording described the landscape. It showed a large panorama of tall structures, taller than the Empire State building with traffic moving on wide highways, except the population growth and a lack of support to keep ahead of infrastructure problems tell a different story.

I bragged about seeing the World's Fair at school that got everyone's attention, including my teacher. She offered me an improved grade, if I wrote an essay about it, which was no small task. I asked everyone in the family what they thought to help me complete the assignment. John was quick to say he was impressed with future building developments, while it convinced Mike the Depression was over. Paul wrote that many important medical breakthroughs were ahead. Pete said the Fair was an example of how much better life was going to be in the future.

I felt the same after seeing the Fair.

Finally, I asked my father what he thought. With his limited insight, he said the present day was more important than the future, ignoring the Fair's theme. I was surprised, since he had been to the Fair with me, but I could understand his thinking. Living one day at a time had been his survival mechanism, especially when he first arrived in America.

Pete suggested we should meet in 1960 to see if the Fair fulfilled our predictions, but when the time came, we were too scattered to discuss twenty year old opinions. During one of my visits, I had to remind my father that he agreed to go over what we discussed. I felt it would be significant, but I wondered what he would say.

He was born a decade before the start of the 20ᵗʰ Century, but his early years were troublesome. I was curious over what it all meant to him. He had experienced world changing events, such as the Great Depression, two World Wars, many medical advancements and domestic changes, including automobiles, airplanes, air conditioning and television.

They were all relevant developments.

The Fair remained a vivid memory to me and I was anxious to ask my father what he thought about it, except he had little recollection of what was said twenty years before.

"What did I say?"

"You said the present day was more important than the future."

"That's right."

"Why," I asked, "Didn't you believe life would be better for you in America?"

"In the beginning, I was worried," he said, "but when I married Mom and had a steady job, as well as a family, everything was good, except I never got rich," he laughed.

I nodded my understanding as he summed up his life. He was not an ambitious man searching for wealth. It was enough for him to take pride in what his children had accomplished, which was all he needed to feel successful. Many parents are proud to cite the accomplishments of their children that represent the achievement of their lives.

It was not unusual.

The only advice my father imparted to us was to be honest, work hard, be polite and a good listener, which was what he learned in America. To fulfil his dream, he lived one day at a time, as he watched the advances of his children do what he never could accomplish, but he lived a life with few regrets.

I soon wished the future was already here, but ominous times lurked ahead. At first, the Fair seemed to blot out another foreign upheaval, but England and France were already at war with Germany. There were strong objections about entering the conflict, but the attack on Pearl Harbor changed those views. America became a part of a devastating war on two fronts. One was in Europe against Germany and the other in the Pacific against Japan.

Nothing more occurred in the ensuing years for my family that was significant, only the normal events of life, some good and some bad, except for the wars. Mostly, I regretted never taking my parents to visit their homeland, except we learned that my father's village in the Lemko region had been destroyed after World War II, including his church.

After living in a city most of their lives and working for Standard Oil for forty one years, my father retired and bought a house in Ocean County, NJ, close to a town where they could walk to shop for food and essentials. My mother was pleased. They used a cart to lug goods home, but were also helped by neighbors that eased their problem for them to tote food. My brothers often visited them to shop for food that would last them at least a week.

I would often help with my visits.

Their house lot was large enough for my father to grow several vegetables in a garden that enabled him to fulfil his longing to return to a rural life. It was a contest between my father's vegetable garden and my mother's flowers.

My father lived to be eighty eight, and my mother passed away five years later at ninety two. They were together for sixty seven years and are buried in an Orthodox cemetery in Cassville, NJ, among many other Rusyns in an area called Rova Farms.

I am the only remaining member of my parents' family. In addition to my mother and father, I have lost my four brothers, John, Mike, Paul and Pete and their wives, Sue, Marie, Dorothy and Virginia. At times, it is hard to reconcile being the youngest with the passing of everyone in my family.

John became a successful house builder in Florida. Mike worked for New York's Transportation Department. Paul was a doctor in Florida near John. Pete lived in New Jersey and sold steel to construct commercial buildings.

I had a career in journalism and advertising, but primarily in the latter. Until recently, my wife and I split our time in New Jersey and Florida, but we now live only in New Jersey. We have two daughters and our son, who are successful in their own endeavours and lucky to have eight grandchildren. All are a joy to my wife and I, but I don't want to give the impression that everything has been rosy. We have experienced many of the twists and turns that occur in any family. The toughest was lost of an infant child.

Mostly, I miss the happy experiences of my life, but many memories remain vivid. There are not many first generation descendants of immigrant parents, who came to America during the early 1900's. In a way, I think it is a special distinction, but I want to emphasize we were fortunate my parents made the journey to America.

Events often seem ordinary in personal histories and this story is no exception. Or am I wrong? Are the experiences of immigrant parents unique? I doubt it, not in America. Finally, the only thing left for me is to repeat my father's favorite phrase.

"Thanks, God."

Author's Notes

The Great Depression of the 1930's was an important time in the country's history and for my family. I concentrated on that era in this book, but I also wanted to tell the story of my parents' heritage and their coming to America. Their meeting and marriage in America made it possible for me and my brothers to build on their efforts, but I also included pertinent insight into their migration.

I have to point out that it often took more time to research parts of the book than it did to write it. I felt it was important to document facts I did not experience. I verified a great deal at the Jersey City History Section at the Main Public Library. It helped to resolve several important issues of the city's early history. I admit that going back over seventy five years was not an easy process, but a rewarding one.

I have told this story through the experiences of my parents and brothers. I tried to relate events in the order they occurred, but at times, it was impossible to hold all the segments to an orderly time period. My only regret is that we lost early pictures of my family and none of my mother survived and few of my father to include in the book.

I researched information on the Prohibition era, as it affected Jersey City and its immigrant population. My brother Mike detailed most of the facts on his gin brewing experience, but John also filled in salient facts. Precise records are not available, but I met with several sources in the Jersey City Police Department on data that goes back over 70 years.

I also met with several residents in downtown neighborhoods that were familiar with the era. I did feel compelled to protect the names throughout the book. I used pseudonyms for several identities, but the events are accurate, as they were related to me. I thought the use of an alias in the chapter on Gin was important, and referenced the researched data that needed to be recorded.

A lot of my brothers' exploits in football are documented, but I also spent time with Harry Jacunski, who played with Paul at Fordham and the Packers. He was effusive on Paul's efforts on the football field, especially in the tie game against Pittsburgh in 1937. I had the same experience with Elmer Angsman, Notre Dame's top running back, who described Pete as both a great blocker on offense and outstanding on defence. All of the data I recorded with a smile.

Lastly, I thought my mother and father's early years in their homeland were important elements of this story. The history of the Rusyn people is difficult to record, but they have shown exceptional resiliency. They were an oppressed people living in extreme poverty, often in the midst of political upheaval that was not of their making. They faced disappointment and despair, as well as a forced dispersal of a portion of their population. The record of their hardships remains a testament to their determination and resolve.

An important fact is that the Carpatho-Rusyn Society members have great respect for their heritage, as well as an unyielding appreciation for the journey their parents and grandparents made by their migration from Eastern Europe to America. It was one thing to leave home, but another to leave families, as many of them had to do, including my father.

Historians are quick to list the names of Rusyns who have achieved success in America, including, the former Governor of Pennsylvania, Tom Ridge and the actor Robert Urich, as well as their favorite artist, Andy Warhol. The history of Rusyns is broader than the few names we are often prone to cite, but they have been contributing in many professions throughout America starting from 1880.

A lot of the credit for expanding the record of Rusyns, as well as the broader task of their history throughout America and Eastern Europe goes to John Reghetti, the founder of the Carpato-Rusyn Society and those who have served in their organizations. The work of the Society's record in America, Canada and Europe deserve more than ordinary recognition. Their efforts expanded the knowledge about an interesting ethnic people.

Through the extended work of the members of the Carpatho-Rusyn Society, there are now Rusyns serving in political offices in countries throughout Eastern Europe, when once there were none. What the Society members have been able to accomplish are important advancements for a people left without a country, but still proud to proclaim their heritage.

Today, almost 700,000 people in the U.S. can trace their history to ancestors who migrated to America. The largest number occurred from the 1880's to the early 1920's. Spend one day at Ellis Island and you will learn about the monumental task immigrants faced to establish themselves in America, especially if they did not speak English, as most of the immigrants from Eastern Europe did not.

There are many nationalities that made the journey to America. The length of the number of Rusyns is far from the top of the list, which makes me feel my parents' migration was extraordinary.

Researching data on my parents' early life helped me understand the problems they faced coming to America to make a better life. In simple words, it was far from easy. Sometimes, I wonder how they were able to do it. I never knew either of my grandparents, but I'm grateful that they had the insight to recognize the opportunity America offered to send their children, my parents to America. Lastly, I realize that the descendants of immigrants all have stories to tell and this is only one of them.

References

Chapter 1: Bright Street. (A) . . . the street was near Paulus Hook, the city's first settlement. Source: "The History of Paulus Hook," by Adele Tamburo. Jersey City: Past and Present. Publisher: The New Jersey Department of Cultural Education.

(B) . . . a fort was built at the settlement . . . by the British . . . George Washington ordered an attack to retake the fort,,, it was repelled. Source: Ibid.

(C) Aaron Burr often rowed across the river to visit a girlfriend in the community. Source: "Burr," Gore Vidal, Random House.

(D) The average blue collar worker earned less than $12 a week (in the 1930's). Source: Kingwood College Library.

(E) . . . unemployment reached twenty five per cent (in the 1930's). Source: Ibid.

(F) . . . the jobless lived in tin shacks called "Hoovervilles." Source: Ibid.

(G) It was "hard times". Source: "Hard Times" An Oral History of the Great Depression by Studs Terkel, Publisher of The New Press.

(H) By the 1930's the city had grown into an active industrial community. Source: "Jersey City Today," published by the Jersey City Division of Communication.

(I) . . . hang in there." Source: Phrase by D. Mitchell, HubPages.com.

The phrase was first used in 1826 by the French Inventor, Niecephore Niepce, who took a picture of his cat, "Croissant," hanging from a silk rope. It required eight hours to get the look and pose he wanted, but Niepce kept encouraging the cat to "hang in there." Posters with the cat and the phrase were prominent during the Depression.

Chapter 2: The Decision. (A) . . . in World War I Rusyn) area was listed in the Austro Hungarian Empire on both sides of the Carpatian Mountains. Source: "Our People," Dr. Paul Robert Magocsi, Universiy of Toronto.

(B) . . . an obscure ethnic people . . . but with a history that can be traced back over a thousand years. Source: Ibid.

(C) The land was known as "Rus." Source: Ibid.

(D) . . . overrun many times by Tartars, Austrians and Poles, Source: John Reghetti, Carpatho Rusyn Society, Pittsburgh, Pa.

(E) . . . in the 9th Century, Rusyns became a part of the Eastern Orthodox Church. Source: Ibid.

(F) . . . centuries later . . . (Rusyn) prelates agreed to accept the Papal authority in Rome . . . but retained important perquisites of the Orthodox Church . . . Source: Ibid.

(G) . . . important development occurred with the acquisition of Eastern Europe by the Austro-Hungarian Empire . . . including area of the Carpathian Mountains. Source: Wikipedia.Org/Galicia/Eastern Europe.

(H) . . . Franz Joseph . . . (Emperor) . . . instituted positive changes. Rusyns called him the Savior. Source: John Reghetti, Carpatho-Rusyn Society, Pittsburgh, Pa.

(I) . . . in World War I, Rusyns were drafted into the Austrian army. Source: Wikipedia. Org/Galicia/ Eastern Europe.

(J) . . . Rusyns were ordered to Ukraine to do farm labor . . . the move was contrived . . . called by the name of a river . . . Operation Vistula. Source: John Reghetti, Carpatho-Rusyn Society, Pittsburgh, Pa.

(K) . . . Rusyns know plan was Communist managed (families were forced to Ukraine) Source: Ibid.

(L) Scholars believe the mountain terrain formed the sturdy character of the people. Source: "Our People," Dr. Paul Robert Magocsi, University of Toronto.

(M) Rusyns cared little about politics and had no nationalistic desires . . . they were peasants . . . living on small plots. Source: John Reghetti, Carpatho-Rusyn Society, Pittsburgh, Pa.

(N) . . . they persevered and farmed the land . . . growing simple crops. Source: "Encyclopedia of Rusyn History and Culture." Dr. Paul Robert Magosci and Ivan Pop.

(O) Some did seasonal labor on large farms in the Eastern plains. Source: Ibid.

(P) . . . early records are sketchy . . . Rusyns were listed below the economic average of most people throughout Europe. Source: "Our People," Dr. Paul Robert Magosci, University of Toronto.

(Q) There were no large markets . . . or mineral deposits . . . as there had been. Source: John Reghetti, Carpatho-Rusyn Society, Pittsburgh, Pa.

(R) The basic strength of the people hinged on their Orthodox beliefs . . . the church was their focal point. Source: Ibid.

(S) . . . priests were their counselors . . . but the people came to view the clergy as part of the upper class. Source: Ibid.

(T) . . . opportunity for workers came from American industry . . . needed in steel mills and coal mines. Source: Ellis Island lecturer.

(U) . . . financial support and aid was provided for immigrants willing to make the journey . . . a $30 ticket for Steerage Class. Source: Ibid.

Chapter 4: Arrival. (A) In less than twenty years, the open door immigration policy would be halted by Congressional edict. Congress passed the Emergency Quotas Act in 1920, followed by the Immigration Act of 1924 to restrict the immigration. Source: Ellis Island brochure.

(B) . . . originally, the Registry Room had no seating, but later there were long rows of benches . . . Source: Ibid.

Chapter 6: New Friends. Jersey City had a large, growing immigrant population. Source: "Jersey City of Today," Jersey City Division of Communication.

Chapter 7: The Coal Mines. (A) . . . there were mule drivers and "buttys" . . . as helpers were called. Source: "Information Guide," Pennsylvania Anthracite Heritage Museum, Scranton, Pa.

(B) Shabby houses . . . called "the patch" . . . a group of miners' homes. Source: Ibid.

Chapter 8: (A) New Start. (A) . . . a 1900 report . . . life expectancy was only forty seven years. Source: Kingwood College Library. "The American Cultural History—1900-1909."

(B) . . . immigrant workers were a plentiful labor supply . . . meager earnings were the norm. There was no minimum wage. The law . . . was passed in 1934 at 0.25 cents per hour. Source: Ibid.

(C) A speed limit of 20 miles per hour was posted in twenty states, but there was less than 100 miles of paved roads. Source: Ibid.

(D) Americans were singing . . . Sweet Adeline . . . listening to it on their RCA Victrola. Source: Ibid.

(E) Carrie Nation was on a crusade, swinging her famous axe in bars. Source: Ibid.

(F) . . . eating at bars . . . free sandwiches were available for ten cent price of a shot of whiskey and a beer. Source: Wikipedia.Org.

(G) . . . a dramatic increase in the pay of Ford Assembly Line Workers . . . from $2.50 to $5.00 . . . but Ford threatened to take away their job if they failed to keep pace. Source: Worker on Assembly Line.

Chapter 9: Anna. (A) . . . scanned immigrants, looking for physical handicaps. Source: Ellis Island Education and Research Center, Health and recorded Immigration: "Ellis Island Museum Family History."

(B) . . . many Rusyns migrated to America. Source: Ellis Island official's estimate.

(C) Immigrants had an immediate need to earn money: Ellis Island Guide.

Chapter 11: Listen and Learn. (A) . . . a product of an ignored peasantry . . . an elementary education did not exist in poor rural areas of Eastern Europe and in America. Source: Wikipedia, Org: Education data on Eastern Europe.

Chapter 12: A Job and a Fire. (A) Jersey City was booming... the population was near 250,000 . . . predictions it would reach a million. Source: Jersey City of Today. Publisher: Jersey City's Division of Communication.

(B) . . . immigrant labor force was nearly 70,000 . . . almost one third of the city's entire population. Source: Ibid.

Chapter 13: The Roarin' 20's. (A) . . . in the 1920's jobs were plentiful and easy spending was the norm. Source: Wikipedia.Org.

(B) In Jersey City . . . for lunch . . . cafes included nonalcoholic drinks, but at night alcoholic drinks were included with dinner. Source: E. Assats Wright of the Hudson Reporter.

(C) It did not stop bootleggers from bringing liquor into the country . . . sold in illegal bars, called "speakeasies." Source: Kingwood College Library, "American Cultural History, 1920-1929."

(D) . . . liquor was hidden in soldiers' boots to bring alcohol into camp . . . which was the origin of the term bootlegger. Source: Wikipedia.Com.

(E) . . . booze, a word immigrants liked. The word refers to an alcoholic drink of hard liquor first used in English in the 14th Century. Source: Words at Random by Dora Wilmot.

(F) . . . the beginning of mass production . . . Henry Ford installed an assembly line for to speed up auto production. Source: Kingwood College Library, "American Cultural History, 1920-1929.

(G) Charles Lindbergh made his solo flight to Paris. Babe Ruth established a home run record. The Four Horsemen of Notre Dame and Red Grange of Illinois excited football fans. Source: Ibid.

(H) . . . flat recorded discs were being produced that played music on a record player . . . the Charleston became the most favorite dance . . . young women called "flappers" doing the dance. Source: Ibid.

(I) . . . a new vernacular was introduced that was a basis of the nature of the 1920's. Source: Time Life Books. "The Jazz Age: The 20's."

Chapter 14: The Thirties: (A) Depression was worse when the pay of many workers was cut in half . . . Source: Kingwood College Library, "the American Cultural History, 1930-1939."

Chapter 19: Mike's Gin Adventure (A) . . . liquor was being smuggled in from Canada and trucked to Red Bank on the Jersey Shore. Source: "Prohibition in New Jersey: Past and Present.

(B) The process to brew gin required a variety of spices . . . Source: Wikipedia. Org/ bathtub gin.

(C) Coriander seeds are used to hide the harsh taste of gin. Source: Ibid.

(D) Juniper berries were a vital additive that gave gin its unique flavor. Source: Ibid.

(E) . . . the banning of liquor sales helped make bathtub gin acceptable. Source: Kingwood College Library. "American Cultural History, 1920-1929."

(F) . . . when bathtub gin was combined with coca cola it camouflaged the harsh taste and dark color of gin. Source: Wikipedia.Org.

(G) . . . gin ingredients are called flavorings. Source: Ibid.

Chapter 20: First Football Game. (A),,, Boyle's Thirty Acres was site of Jack Dempsey's championship fight against Georges Carpentier in 1921. Source: Jersey Journal. "The Day History Was Made in Jersey City." Ed Brennan, Jan. 9, 1960.

Chapter 22: The Seven Blocks of Granite. (A) . . . their 1936 game ended in another scoreless tie. Source: Wikipedia.org.

(B) Grantland Rice . . . report on the game stated: "The Fordham line still stands." Source: Ibid.

(C) Fordham's Sports Information Director Tim Cohane wanted a more compelling name. Source: Ibid.

(D) . . . ten players over two seasons to produce its defensive record. They all have clear credentials as members of the Seven Blocks of Granite. Source: Jack Newcombe, Saga Magazine. 1960.

(E) "Fordham versus Pittsburgh 1937) was the school's Finest Hour. Source: Ibid.

(F) Jack Dempsey wished the team good luck. Source: The New York Times.

(G) Johnny Druze, Fordham's . . . captain and place kicker missed three field goal attempts . . . one he said he should have made. Source: Johnny Druze on the 1937 tie game.

(H) . . . 1938 game, Jock Sutherland, Pittsburgh's coach . . . said Paul's performance was outstanding. Source: Pittsburgh Stops Fordham on October 30,1938 Pittsburgh Post Gazette.

(I) Marshall Goldberg . . . selected Paul to his All Opponent team. Source: Goldberg Picks his Team. November 11. 1938. Pittsburgh Post Gazette.

(J) Sutherland named to coach Eastern College All Stars against the New York Giants . . . picks Paul as one his tackles. Source: November 15, 1938. Ibid.

Chapter 25: Mike – Hero and Renegade. (A) . . . he would sing a song about the hardships of the road. Source: Joel (Joe Hill) Hoogland song, "Hallelujah, I'm a bum." First (performed} publically in early 1900's. Source: Wikipedia.Org.

Chapter 33: World of Tomorrow. (A) . . . It produced an extraordinary force of citizens to combat a Depression, as well to win a major war. Source: Tom Brokaw, from his book, "America's Greatest Generation.

(B) Several Government programs were passed in 1934 that was the start of America's Middle Class. Source: Norman Ornstein, Author and a Political Analyst of the American Enterprise Institute. Data was presented by Norman Ornstein on MSNBC.